Stealing the Ambassador

a novel

Sameer Parekh

THE FREE PRESS

Published by Simon & Schuster

New York   London   Toronto   Sydney   Singapore

_f_P

THE FREE PRESS
A Division of Simon & Schuster, Inc.
1230 Avenue of the Americas
New York, NY 10020

First Free Press trade paperback edition 2003
THE FREE PRESS and colophon are trademarks of Simon & Schuster Inc.
For information regarding special discounts for bulk purchases, please contact Simon & Schuster Special Sales at 1-800-456-6798 or business@simonandschuster.com

Designed by Karolina Harris
Manufactured in the United States of America

10 9 8 7 6 5 4 3 2 1

The Library of Congress has cataloged the Free Press edition as follows:
Parekh, Sameer.
Stealing the ambassador : a novel / Sameer Parekh.
p. cm.
1. India—History—20th century—Fiction. 2. Fathers and sons—Fiction. 3. Grandfathers—Fiction. 4. Sabotage—Fiction. I. Title.
PS3616.A74 S74 2002
813'.6—dc21   2001050157

ISBN: 978-0-7432-1430-8

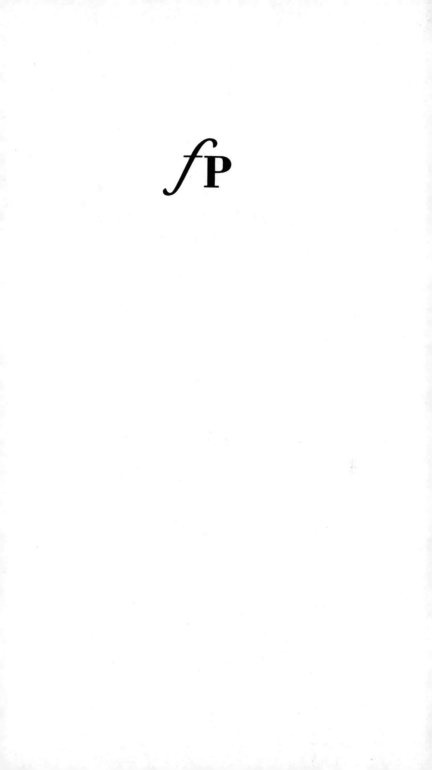

For my parents

And I told them I was writing about him then, and they told me some of their truths, and secret lies, just as Jack had, and his wife Alice and his lovely light o' love, Kiki, had years ago. I liked all their lies best, for I think they are the brightest part of anybody's history.

—WILLIAM KENNEDY

Stealing the Ambassador

There's an old story in my family.

It starts at night. We are in northwest India, in a minor city of mud-brown brick and gray stone. Fields, newly green, surround and sprawl from the city, extending into the night, filling the space between this place and the next. In this city there is a university and near the university there are rows of small and square houses. Each house has four windows made with panes of heavy and uneven glass. The glass warps and twirls the views into the homes and out to the streets.

Behind one of these windows, in one of these houses, in the center of a room, there is a sheet, powder blue, spread across a section of floor covered with tiles. At one end of this room there is a door to a bedroom. From here my grandfather, my father's father, emerges, lengths of paper resting along his outstretched arms. He moves slowly. His look is serious, his eyes are wide, his clothing is plain white cotton.

He is young, like I've never seen him, but imagine this worn black-and-white photo I have infused with Technicolor. His skin is a warm brown, darker and firmer than my own hue. He is thin, his hair and his eyes are black. His clean-shaven face is made of hard edges everywhere except for his eyes and his ears, which are both large and soft. He smiles a big smile as he sits. Spreading his burden on the sheet, he is meticulous, allowing for no wrinkles in the papers that will set the course of his life. There are three men besides my grandfather seated on this sheet, and they are less reverent with these blueprints and surveys. My grandfather is the shortest of the lot and sitting, watching, his face is closest to the prints. Seen through the window, his cross-legged frame, a contour clothed in white, resolves itself into the papers, and as the other men push and pull at them, his body sways and crackles.

My grandmother enters through the other door, the one opposite the bedroom. She is holding a tray with five cups of tea, each placed on a saucer, and a teapot, large enough to fill each of the cups once again. I am not sure how she looks; we don't have a photo of her at this age. Everyone says my aunt takes after her, so imagine my grandmother to be thin and short, not quite five feet, less than one hundred pounds. She is fifteen or sixteen. She wears a dark blue sari. Her eyes and hair are dark and though her skin is lighter than her husband's, she knows that she is not fair enough to be a real beauty. Still, she's pretty, with a round face and discreet eyes. Serving the men first, she takes the final cup and saucer and moves to sit beside my grandfather. Adjusting her sari, she sips her tea. She remarks on the men's discussion with enough frequency and acumen that we come to understand she is not an outsider to this process, that she understands the practicalities involved in bombing a bridge.

Before a quarter of an hour has passed, she has finished her drink. She continues to sit. If she does not blend into the papers as her husband does, her sari at least complements the sheet, harmonizing in tones of blue, part of the conspiracy.

It is August and rain feels imminent. Outside and inside the air is wet. Insects swim through the miasma, pretending they are flying. They leak into the room, one after another, through open windows and doors not quite shut, attracted by the fragile oil-lamp light. Soon our group sits in the middle of a chorus of pests. No person is disturbed, so intent are they. They are singing too, these conspirators, humming, their mouths and tongues, their hair, their bodies, vibrating with immoderate passion. Their blue sheet is a magic carpet and the passing flies and mosquitoes and gnats are only proof that they are flying.

This all happened two days before the bridge tumbled. Professionally, the group was unqualified. My grandfather was a lecturer in law at the university. One of the other men taught mathematics. My grandmother was a wife, and the remaining two men, cousins, were cloth merchants. One of the men, the mathematician, I think, figures where to place the bombs. The merchants get the explosives from a contact involved in silver mining. My grandfather sees to it that the bombing is well timed and convenient in all possible considerations. My grandmother keeps my grandfather balanced.

Two days pass before the story resumes. It's still night but this time there is rain, orchestrated, falling with intent and direction, descending in great, full swells. The swells are a collective crescendo, each more powerful than the last, and it seems the monsoon is in danger of expending its ardor in the space of this one night. Four men are walking beside a river, twenty miles from town, north, toward the bridge they will bomb. From where we sit, one can't be distinguished from the next, brown men in black, so damp they are liquid, ebbing and flowing among one another.

When the bombs go off, after caring placement prescribed by the mathematician, only these four bear witness. There are three blasts, one after another, that are overwhelmed by the continuing quiet of night, and though after the third explosion there is a creak, the superstructure of the bridge does not seem shaken. The teacher of mathematics is concerned. He runs up and down the riverbank, examining the bridge from different angles, willing it to fall, imploring the gods of calculation.

Perhaps this works. The silence that follows the creak is interrupted by the sound of a first crack, then after that a second. Then there are a hundred small cracks and the noise is that of a string of firecrackers to the men, the long fuse finally burned, the excitement and fury begun.

Against a background of cracking, bones of timber detach themselves, defeated, and fall to the water. Downstream, these four men watch as fractions of the span wash by them, carried away by a river which may or may not have been swiftly flowing at the time. On this point I'm ill informed.

There is a second part to the story, a getaway. The four men return home, spent after their tryst. Sleeping, they ease back into their familiar selves. My grandfather does not wake till past noon on the following day. He washes and eats, then walks to the university to collect his mail. On the streets and in the mailroom there is talk; the mail has not arrived this morning. On his way home he takes the longer way, the longest way, stopping on a hill overlooking the civil lines.

To his eye, the place seems to gather and disperse in an accelerated meter. To his ear, there is more shouting, more cursing, though from his vantage none of the words are clear. He stays there till dusk watching these pale white people as they move in and out of their square brick buildings, sometimes to still-greater offices, with bigger arches and higher walls, sometimes to smaller, less impressive structures.

He comes home to eat. My grandmother serves him. When he has finished his meal he fills his glass with water from an earthenware pot that sits just outside the kitchen. He finds the newspaper and comes to rest in a chair, reading, while my grandmother serves herself. She eats and when she has finished she says, "I think a great many people know who did this."

He responds. "A great many people do not know. Very few people know, if that many."

"I think they may know. This is not your fault." She softens her statement, defending him with her voice and her look so that he might hear her.

"Why do you think so many people know?"

"There has been a good deal of talk."

"There will be talk." He thinks before he says, "London Bridge will not fall without people talking." He looks again at his newspaper, then at her, at the paper again. "Who?"

"My friends think it was you." She looks at the floor. At her feet.

"Then they must think it was you, too." He smiles, amused. "They must think you knew about it."

Through the uneven window glass, the rutted, dusty lane that runs in front of this small university house looks, to her, like an earthen wave, rising and falling, about to crash. She does not smile as she says, "They think this also." My grandmother is worried; this is clear to my grandfather, finally.

"Your friends are guessing only, to pass the time. To tease you." He reaches to embrace her. "It is nothing. Come."

She evades his grasp, gathering the vessels, piling

them, one on top of another, balancing them as she takes them into the kitchen. She says in a loud voice, so that he can hear her as she moves away, "It is something, it is talk, and a great many people are talking."

He calls after her, "It is women passing time!" His hair is combed across his head, from left to right, in straight, insistent lines.

"Women pass time with men also." She is steady, framed in the doorway to the kitchen. Her black hair is pulled back from her forehead. Her *bindi* glares, revealed like a third eye.

"What will men do with gossip? Laugh, perhaps. And if they believe, what then? They will not tell, they are our people."

"Whose people are they?" She has returned to the room and stands above her husband as she asks the question.

"Ours. Our people. They are Indian."

"They are not so Indian, all of them. They are not so Indian, these Indians of yours."

But he has begun to convince her. She is less concerned—worried still, but appeased. My grandfather puts down his paper and holds her. Later she washes the dishes she has taken into the kitchen while my grandfather stands behind her, pulling at her sari, singing her a love song.

She is right, of course. Within two days one of the cloth merchants is arrested. He is at home. The police have tracked the sale of the explosives. His wife, who did not know beforehand of his involvement, is confused. Though the merchant imagined himself brave, at this moment he is only frightened and apologetic.

His daughter is young, five or six, and while one policeman sits in the drawing room, explaining to the merchant that he will be arrested for the bombing, she plays games with another on the front stoop. She takes the dull olive beret from off his head, runs into the courtyard that extends from the lowest of the steps, and throws the headpiece back at him. This second policeman smiles and plays along, as though he were an uncle or a cousin, replacing his beret each time so the game may be commenced anew.

My grandmother learns of the arrest before my grandfather. When he returns from the university she has already packed two bags, tightly and efficiently. My grandfather's brother, who lives in the same house, enters and is surprised by their packing, the restive feel of their greetings. The brother is, at this time, the lesser luminary. A lawyer also, he is unremarkable. He is without knowledge of the bridge and the bombing. When my grandfather explains to him, he is precise.

"The railway bridge, bombed three nights ago, was bombed by me. With others, too, but I was involved."

"Which bridge? The one which was just bombed? That was you?"

"Not just bombed. Three nights past. That was partly my doing."

"I see."

"They've arrested one of us already. He will tell them who helped him. I'm going to hide in Bombay for some time, until I think of what better to do."

"Bombay. Good, good. A maze there. No one will find you there."

"This is what I was thinking. I know some people to stay with. I can grow a beard and a mustache and all that nonsense."

"A proper disguise. Very good." He slaps my grandfather on the back, beaming.

"Help us pack." My grandmother has been gathering together necessities while my grandfather has been explaining.

"Of course, yes."

They are ready within the hour. My grandfather says good-bye to his brother first. He is alone with my grandmother, his wife. He brushes her cheek, promising to be in touch soon, explaining no harm will come to him. He will sort through this and before long—a week, a month, perhaps—they can meet in Bombay and go elsewhere. His plan is very reasonable.

When the police come they are crisp and sterile. Learning that my grandfather is away, lost to them, they arrest instead my grandmother. The merchant remembered her to the authorities, sitting with them, serving them tea, talking on occasion. Even as my grandmother stands before the police, she is falling. It

all seems very unreasonable now, this unexpected egal-
itarianism, this respect for her small role. She faints.
When she is revived, her situation is the same. In her
house, she is arrested. Under interrogation she is sure
she does not know where my grandfather is. At trial she
is sentenced to three years in a women's prison. Neither
of the two solicitors she knows is in the courtroom to
hear her sentence delivered.

My grandfather's brother, too, is arrested. More on a
whim than for any discernible reason, he is held for
questioning and beaten. For twelve days he suffers, but
not once does he mention Bombay. When he is released
he is admitted to a hospital, where he heals. Again well,
he has missed my grandmother's trial, but visits her in
prison, promising to agitate as my grandfather would
have liked. He becomes an important local politician, a
firebrand, respected and known.

My grandfather comes to visit his wife after three
months, disguised as her brother. They talk for just one
hour; she promises him that she will be well and smiles
so that he believes her. She will pass the time and he
will continue to hide.

In the next two years he fells eight more bridges,
alone, avoiding capture. His wife, sentenced to three
years, is released in two. He meets her at her parents'
home and together they move to a new city under new
names, newlyweds once more. He bombs no more
bridges. In time they will start a family.

❊

It is a good story as stories go. For a child it is the perfect sort of story, engaging and romantic, a circumscribed and accessible history, populated with personal heroes. I'd lose myself in it, playing one brother then the other, always appreciative of the heroine, the virtue and the bravery and the love. But the story may be half told. I've heard that my grandfather knew of his wife's imminent arrest. His brother told where my grandfather was hidden, screaming "Bombay" till he collapsed, unconscious, from the pain. This might have occurred, too. My grandmother does not speak to my grandfather any longer; they pass each other as they might have before they were married and cast in this epic.

And me, the audience, I've become a thief. I cracked open a man's skull to get the car I'm now driving, an aging Ambassador. As I try to manage the clutch and the gears and the subcontinental traffic, to steer a way clear through this mess, I find myself thinking in circles: the story, the bridge, my grandfather, his son, my father, his mother, my grandmother, her husband, his brother. Again the story. I became a thief for a cause, for the story, I think.

ne

i.

In 1966 my father was born for a second time in this, his most recent life, baptized by a gentle and lazy January snowfall, flake after flake, a thousand perfect welcomes, he remembered aloud once, to a new country. When he woke the next day, snow covered the earth in swells and valleys of unbroken, unrelenting white, and my father thought, because he had, hours ago, been on a plane for the first time, if you could steal the clouds from the sky and spread them over the earth, neatly, evenly, this is what it would look like. To hear him tell it, before he'd ever seen a spring or summer or fall, he'd found a favorite season.

He mentioned his arrival to me once. I was eleven, sitting with my parents and my brother on folding chairs at the dinner table. "Oh, I liked it, that is for certain." My father's English was accented, a thick and general auditory reminder that his passport had once been Indian. To those more attuned to such nuances, his speech said northern, not southern, India, his grammar an obvious clue that his schooling had been Gujarati, not English medium. This night, like most nights, he jumped between the two. "This is not to say, of course, that the winter liked me. Think on it. I had only two suits when I came here. One blue, one gray, neither wool. And only one coat that was much too thin. Less than adequate."

As my father spoke, his right hand would tear at the *roti* and use it to collect *subzi* in an off-centered cone of bread and vegetable. This he'd dip into a bowl of *daal*, so the structure was moistened and flavored, and then feed himself. His left hand would gesticulate like a drunken butterfly, flapping, soaring then falling, attentive always to his story. I remember friends showing me they could pat their heads and rub their bellies at the same time and theirs seemed mean feats.

The immensity of that first winter overwhelmed him. With two suits and a coat he was always on the edge of cold, always aware that he was bothered. He supplemented money from his graduate student grant by working part-time at a small shoe store, nine to six on Saturday, twelve to five on Sunday, off the books. He alternated between his suits and hoped the knees of his pants didn't wear thin. Laughing, on another night, he said, "The craziness of Americans. Their whole day was make or break if they do or don't find the right shoes. They made me the responsible party." He folded his hands together and pressed them against his forehead in mock supplication. "*Arre baba,* it's not my fault. My job is to squat down, measure your feet, to stand up, to get your shoes, to put them on your feet, and then to package them all again when none suit you. This only. For manufacturing, this is not my department. Talk to Florsheim, sahib."

That next winter he used the money he'd saved to buy a coat, orange and down-filled, the pick of the Salvation Army's litter. Short and slight, the coat doubled half of him, making his torso seem a burden too large for his thin legs. He appeared, from a distance, to wobble as he walked down streets. He was warm, though, and he made it a point to roam about when wiser folk stayed indoors.

He got mittens, a scarf, and a hat. He learned the difference between slush and sleet, between wet and dry snow, about snowmen and toboggans. He bought a shovel, enjoying the banter with neighbors who were also awake early, clearing front steps and sidewalks. He decided that four inches of snow was the right amount, not too great an obstruction, significant enough to turn the city beautiful.

When he was done talking that night his left hand would have fallen to the table, exhausted, and his right might have reached for a glass of water. He'd drink in long swallows, his throat sliding up and down inside his neck like a hurried earthworm. When he'd finished, the glass would have been marked by the oil and ghee of my mother's cooking, pressed by the tips of my father's fingers into five patterns, unique the whole world over.

Twenty-five months after he came from India, my father graduated with a master's in electrical engineering from the Newark College of Engineering and landed a job with a computer company in upstate New York. After a year with the company he flew home to India, in February 1969. My grandfather and grandmother had been inquiring and conducting interviews. When he arrived, my father chose my mother from the six options his parents offered. They spent an hour together, chaperoned, and my mother and father decided they were both agreeable to the match. They married three weeks later, in a ceremony surprisingly large given the time constraints involved.

After the wedding, the new couple, and my father's mother and father, and my father's younger brother, piled into a brand-new Ambassador with a driver and began a weeklong honeymoon, just the six of them. They visited Rajasthan, paying particular attention to temples along the way. At the end of the week my father flew back to America and returned to work. My mother lived with my father's family for the next four months, until her visa was ready and her packing done. In June she landed at JFK and my father picked her up, wondering what to say.

I was born six years later. Four years after that, they had my brother. Two months before that second birth, the three of us moved out of our one-bedroom apartment into a raised ranch, upstate, far enough from New York City that real estate prices were manageable. My father and mother shared one bedroom, my younger brother and I shared another, and it was the third room, the smallest of the three, nine by ten with an old green carpet and a small closet, through which my father's family, thirteen people in all, spread mattresses and blankets and pillows on the floor and arrived in a new country.

They came in two and threes, following my father to America. Some had always wanted to come; some came because they had failed in India. I was twelve when they started to arrive.

First came my father's older sister, my aunt and her husband. He was skinny, she was not. They both found work in the same strip mall, she at Bradlees, in cosmetics, he as a stock boy at Wal-Mart. Together, they made $9.25 an hour and worked eighty hours a week. When they got overtime they'd make time and a half, just about fourteen every hour, and treat themselves to ice cream at Baskin-Robbins before returning home. After dinner they would lose themselves in Hindi films, watching a life of wealth and power from which it seemed they were forever removed, to forget the day they had worked, that tomorrow, they would do the same.

They stayed with us for sixteen months. When they left, back to India to sell their house, their children came to live with us, two sons and a daughter. The two men moved into the spare bedroom and their sister passed the night on a sleeping bag in front of the television, downstairs. I watched shows over her sleeping body that year, the volume so low that I would have to concentrate, rebuilding dialogue from the indistinct contours of actors' voices.

When my aunt and uncle returned they moved in with their daughter to the living room. This is how we lived for the next nine months, the house always filled, growing like an overlush garden, thicker and denser with new lives and new clutter; more shoes at the front door, more towels in the bathroom, more praying, more incense, more coats, more toothbrushes, new brands of toothpaste, new newspapers, saris, *bindis*, till with this new weight, this mass of people, space and time were forced to warp.

The day assumed new cadences. The kitchen table could seat only six people, so the men and my brother and I would eat first, my mother and aunt and her daughter serving us. The men would talk among themselves, my brother and I would talk to each other, the women would feed us until we were full. Afterward, we'd leave the table to them, going downstairs to watch Dan Rather, my father explaining America, referring to the broadcast. When they'd eaten and cleaned the kitchen, the women would come sit with us and we'd all watch on television a pirated cassette rented from the Indian grocery store. By nine-thirty the set was off in deference to my uncle and aunt, tired and in need of sleep. Upstairs, my uncle's two sons would shower, one after the next, readying themselves for work on the night shift. Washing, they'd sing aloud, *filmi* songs, and their voices would carry, over the shower curtain and through the door, down the hall and into the bedroom my brother and I shared, the room where nightly my parents would sequester themselves with their children, resurrecting for a third of an hour the nuclear life they had grown accustomed to since arriving in America.

Waking, again the house was full. My cousins would return from work and eat a meal in the kitchen. My brother and I would get ready for school; my parents, my aunt and uncle and their daughter, would get ready for work. Everyone took lukewarm showers and ate bowls of cereal and despite the rush it seemed that we were all always late.

They moved out, to a two-bedroom apartment in New Jersey. Four months later two more people came, my father's younger brother and his wife. They moved, after half a year, to Jackson Heights. After them came five more: two of my father's nephews for eight months; afterward, an older brother and his wife for a little longer; finally, a niece who stayed for four months, until she was arranged to marry a man from Michigan. Five months after the house emptied I left for college. Four years later I finished and began studying to be a doctor. It was during my first semester in medical school that my father had a heart attack, shoveling snow from the driveway of the house he'd bought in seventy-nine.

My mother drove my father to the hospital, snow be damned. When he'd stabilized and was assigned to the cardiac care unit, my mother sat by his bed, holding her husband's hand as he woke and slept in ten-minute cycles. She left briefly to buy herself a cup of coffee. When she returned she wasn't allowed back into his room. From the hallway, through the glass, she watched, as though it were a silent movie, a cast of stolid doctors and pretty nurses flurry around my father. They slowed and finally stopped and where you might expect the movie to have spliced in a screen of printed dialogue, a white coat opened the door to let my mother know her husband was dead.

Her own father died before I was born, two years after she married. My keenest impression of the person he was comes from my mother's recollection of events at the end of her seventeenth year. She was a senior in high school at an all-girls academy, second in a class of two hundred, when she decided to take the entrance examination for medical school. My mother asked for her parents' permission. Initially reluctant, they acquiesced and through the following four months she studied for the exam. On the evening prior my grandmother arranged for a puja. My mother prayed intently, first for her family's well-being and, afterward, to pass the exam.

Three hundred boys and thirty girls took the statewide test in a too warm auditorium at a local college. In years past, with similar numbers taking the examination, four people were offered admission. My mother sat with the girls in the front two rows of the auditorium. Behind them two rows were left empty and

behind these two rows the boys filled what space remained. The exams were distributed and the room collapsed to the smell of sweat and the sound of pen on
paper. The test lasted six hours. At its end my mother
avoided her friends and hurriedly commandeered a cycle rickshaw to take her home. She cried intermittently
through the night, embarrassed and devastated by how
poorly she knew she had done. She applied, the next
day, for a place in the Bachelor of Commerce class entering the following year. Time passed. She was admitted. Her family convinced her that events had worked
out for the best, because now she could stay at home
while attending college.

Two months later my mother fell ill with malaria. Her
temperature peaked every third day, approaching one
hundred and five degrees each time, and in the days between the fever spikes my mother would lie in bed and
anticipate feeling much worse. She imbibed quinine.
Three days after the fever finally broke, word arrived
that the results had been posted for the medical school
entrance exam. She begged her father not to check her
score but my grandfather insisted to his debilitated
daughter that it was best to confront one's failures
head-on. He sent a man from his office to get the grade.
Later that evening, when my grandfather returned
from work, curiosity had gotten the better of my
mother and she asked him for the score. Her father, his
face tight and serious, told his daughter the results were
not good, that in this case, it was better not to know.

My mother understood her failure must be severe. No one mentioned the examination again. She entered college that August and graduated in three years, in the first division, thoroughly uninterested by her course work. Six months after her graduation she and my father were married and four months after this she came to America to be his wife.

After her first year in America, her father got sick, but not so seriously, she supposed. She called home to speak to him and there was nothing in his voice, she'd recall later, that indicated that he might be about to die. They exchanged pleasantries and gossip till she said good-bye.

"A moment, please," her father said.

"Yes," said my mother.

A moment passed. "Are you happy in America?"

"I am happy," my mother answered, reflexively at first, and then again, with the same words, in a more considered fashion.

My grandfather grunted affirmatively. "Your husband, he is a good husband?"

"Really, Papa," she said, embarrassed.

"Is he?"

"He is good," my mother replied.

She waited again for him to say good-bye. Instead he said nothing and my mother, fearing the line had been disconnected, called "Hello" twice, loudly, into the receiver. My grandfather, his voice delayed, tinny and echoing on the overseas line, said, "You were admitted to medical school. You placed third on the exam. I was proud of you. I decided, however, that you were too sickly to go away to school. Also, I did not think it made sense to educate a girl in that manner. I thought I may have been wrong. But you are happy now, yes? I do not feel I made such a bad decision. I hope that you will feel the same. *Beti*, you cannot change a part of who you are now without changing the whole."

My mother said nothing, weighing the betrayal, twelve thousand miles away and five years removed. "Thank you, Papa," my mother said flatly. Her father waited, trying to gauge the sincerity of her statement. He said good-bye and hung up. They exchanged aerograms dutifully and spoke once again, in taut phrases and long, heavy pauses, before he died.

It is the instinct toward self-preservation that allows me to rationalize his action. Without him there would be no me and my mother would have been part of some other whole. But though I accommodate this deceit, man that he might have been, my mother's father is forever framed for me by this one choice.

My father, to his credit, was incensed by the whole affair and in the months before her father's death pushed my mother to apply to medical school in the States. My mother understood, however, that she didn't have the degree, or the language skills, or the money to go to school, at least not in America. Despite herself she came to advocate her father's decision. Perhaps it was in deference to his memory; more likely, I think, it was because she recognized that to do otherwise would make my father feel like the flat tire that had waylaid her on the road to more exciting times, and he was, after all, her husband.

I don't know what my parents were like when they married. In the photo albums, they seem alive in the thrill of each other's company, and even in those few pictures where one or the other is alone, reading or walking, happiness seems implicit in their carriage and the light in the space around them. It may be that this sort of photo is unavoidable, that at every marriage's onset, it is easy to get the good picture. The world is before them and who might say to the two in the photo that theirs will not be a union for the ages, that their children will not be splendid, that money and happiness are not guaranteed.

Even still, the photos surprise me, because as a child raised in a country that, despite its own troubles managing the institution, marvels skeptically at the notion of an arranged marriage, it was impossible that my parents would not seem slightly suspicious. The dynamics of such a union seemed fraught with potential for mishap. Once you've been married, what next? What do you talk about, what do you want to tell each other? Are trust and affection immediate, like an orphan reunited with his long-lost mother? If not, when does it come, how does one wait?

Though theirs was an arranged marriage it was in many ways an atypical Indian marriage for the time. My parents were alone from the time my mother arrived in the country. They could be private, angry and amorous, silly and intimate, in ways in which their lives in India would not have allowed. I think sometimes that it was these opportunities as much as it was the simple accident of their wedlock that made the photographs luminous.

A stranger probably took my favorite picture of them. They are on the ferry to the Statue of Liberty, which is a distant but distinct blue-green figure in the photo. They are standing, leaning lightly against a white railing, New York Harbor and a summer sky in the background. The wind is blowing wisps of my mother's hair across her face, along her forehead and cheeks. She is wearing sunglasses, the kind Jackie Kennedy wore, and, slight and regally beautiful, she looks very much like an Indian Audrey Hepburn. Kissing her temple and smiling is my father, his nose pressed lightly into the side of her head, the frames of his glasses almost in profile. On either side of them are two white couples, dressed much like my parents, looking at the both of them, smiling approvingly. The rest of the boat is entirely unconcerned.

Another picture, taken by a friend of my father's, is a close second. There were two students, Gujarati like he was, who had completed engineering degrees in the States and with whom my father became close. My father was the first of the three to marry, and in pictures from her first years in the States, my mother is often framed with my father and his friends, the neighborhood tomboy. In this particular picture, the two friends are implied, one as the picture taker, the other a leg and arm along the left edge of the photo. My father and mother are in the picture's center, sitting in the snow, trying to attach chains onto the tires of a white car that must have been their first. My father is sitting cross-legged, looking confused but smiling slightly, the chains lying in his lap, his hands trying to fit part of the tangle over the tire. He is in a long gray overcoat, without a hat, black leather gloves on his hands. My mother is sitting next to him in a blue coat and a blue hat. She is laughing, pointing, her hands gloveless, to a spot on the tire where she presumably thought the apparatus attached. The picture appeals to me because though my father looks confused, he doesn't seem disappointed, only amateurish. The scene seems hopeful, with the excitement of a winter trip to somewhere building, not dissipating. My mother's joy is obvious, a burst of exuberance on her face.

In the year before his death, my father had ceased viewing obstacles as anything less than an affront. He seemed to be fed up with it all, annoyed to frustration that more often than he liked, he couldn't get the chains onto those damned tires. He'd rage about the people at work, about the people in town, about the country in general, about the country in descriptive particulars. He'd wonder aloud about returning to India.

❀

After my father's cremation, relatives stayed on, some for weeks, as if their old rooms needed filling. To close each day, they sang *bhajans*, desperate, perfected appeals to God. Receding into night, the house rang with the sounds of their devotion, and we slept on the warm and raspy vibrations of the harmonium's last note.

But I didn't rest well. I ranged back and forth between sleep and wakefulness, stopping occasionally, en route from one to the other, in a neither-here-nor-there stupor that felt heavy and alcoholic. At some point, during each of these episodes, my father, one, then five, then ten days dead, sat down on my bed. A younger man, twenty pounds lighter, his hair was trimmed into a shined shock of black. He was in a suit, dark gray and smart, and he had on a thin black tie and black horn-rimmed glasses. His face was fresh, his eyes were bright. He'd sit there and I'd lay there, the room frozen more still and brittle than the winter world outside, till he reached down for his suitcase, and was off, out the door.

My father talked of India increasingly as he aged, but was still more excited by Super Bowl parties than by *navratri garbas*, and though most years he took the train into the city on the Fourth, he could never be convinced to attend the India Day parade. He was twenty-four, a year older than I am now, when he arrived in America.

Thirty years later, in November 1998, he was caught in some confused middle; dead of a vegetarian diet that wasn't the least bit healthy, dead in a funeral home in upstate New York, on Washington Street, surrounded by a hundred Indian faces.

We hardly talked in the years preceding his death. We'd try to converse, feeling there was a form to be followed and that fathers and sons ought not be so silent together but, despite our efforts, we were peculiar reagents that produced a collective fizzle, our conversations abortive. I disagreed with him about most things; he wondered how I could think the way I did. In the way a person progresses from a cigarette on weekends to a few cigarettes during the week till all at once he can't remember a time, not so clearly, in any case, when he wasn't a smoker, my father and I learned in increments to be silent, each failure making the next conversation more difficult, until the very notion that we might have anything at all to talk about seemed an idea belonging to our past.

My mother is small and thin and besides the creep of gray over her head, she does not look so different from the pictures of her taken before I was born. She is mild and slow to anger. She is curious but she is cautious in her curiosity. She moderates her expressions, her smiles and her frowns, when she senses someone watching. When, early in the morning, six days after my father died, I walked into the kitchen, she was lost in some private thought and, missing my approach, I caught her face unrestrained and happy.

"Morning, Mom."

"Good morning, *beta,*" she said.

"What were you thinking?"

"Oh, about your father."

"About what?"

"I was remembering that, after my marriage, I would wake in the night, trying to remember my husband's face."

My mother was dressed that morning in a long white cotton nightgown, flowers on the fabric multicolored and minute, faded, too, into a blurry softness by the aggression of rinse and soap and spin. She had a robe on over the gown, heavy and blue, that she had cinched round her waist. She looked, for most of the week after my father's death, antique and worn. Her clothing seemed a protective wrap, to dull jostles from her world before they disturbed her.

"You should understand," she said, continuing, "it is not easy being a new wife. Your father was in America and I was living with his family, my new family. In those days, before we had all come to America, we were seventeen people.

"Everyone was nice, I'm not saying anybody was not nice. But I was trying to remember who liked their tea strong, who liked their *roti* crisp, where all the things were kept, what work needed to be done. I didn't have the time to think on your father."

It was still dark outside. On the panes of the window, behind the plants that sat on the sill behind the kitchen sink, on those plates of glass, crystal fronds of frost had grown overnight, sharp and jagged, new life, almost. My mother made as though to scratch at them, but they were outside and she was inside. She tapped on the window and the arbor remained adherent. My mother shrugged.

"I knew his face, of course. We had wedding photos. But when I would think about him at night, something would happen. His nose would grow or his ears would grow, or he would have a beard. Something. I would try with my mind to give his face that right shape, to give him a shave if that is what he needed. Then, as soon as I fixed one thing, before everything was back to normal, something else would go wrong. I knew what he should look like, but I couldn't imagine him in the right way. I thought it was my failure."

She shook her head, amused at the thought. "What a headache I gave to myself!"

My mother is not a cosmopolitan Indian woman. There are women, her age, Indian, who were raised in those households where worlds of alternate possibility existed for girls. Having missed her shot at medical school, though, my mother was given no option but to locate her aspirations around her family. She stayed at home until I was fourteen and my brother was ten, working part-time as a bookkeeper out of her bedroom, because she felt that a mother's place was, should be, with her children.

It's not so hard to imagine her as a much younger woman, newly arrived in my grandfather's house, practicing her wifely chores so diligently that her husband, newly met, waiting on the other side of the world, was relegated to foggy obscurity. It is even less surprising that almost thirty years removed from the event, it seems to her like a story that involves an altogether different person in a life that, though familiar, can scarcely be believed.

On her first day in this country, my mother met Red Holtzmann, then the coach of the soon-to-be-world-championship New York Knicks. Neither she nor my father discovered this until the next year, 1970, when watching, halfheartedly, the television, they recognized the person on the screen as the man who had taught my mother to eat pizza.

My mother had flown into New York during the early summer of 1969. Too nervous to eat on the plane, she was ravenous by the time she arrived in America. My father, excited to welcome his bride, anxious as well, began to talk and explicate as soon as my mother landed, perhaps to orient her, maybe to settle himself. My mother nodded her head and kept quiet, responding when she was asked a question, unsure of how much detail her husband desired, unsure of what she should and shouldn't be saying. It was not until they had almost reached home that my father asked my mother if she was hungry.

He took her to Frank's Pizzeria and found it closed at four in the afternoon, too late for lunch, too early for dinner. But pressing his face to the glass, he sensed some movement inside and knocked on the window. Frank, big and round, hair on his arms but not on his head, opened the front door and, recognizing my father, said, "What can I do for you, Vasant? It's a little early for dinner, don't you think?"

"This is my wife," said my father, and as Frank turned to my mother she took a step backward. "She has just come from India and she is hungry."

Frank extended his hand, and my father took hold of my mother's forearm and placed it in his friend's callused paw. Frank smiled at my mother and said softly and slowly, "Well, little lady, let's see if I can't make you something that you'll like."

My father said, "Thank you," and the three of them stepped inside.

I'd often wonder what it was about my mother that drew my father to her. His choice, of course, was not made at random: his parents had offered him six options. Still, he could have chosen five other women. Perhaps he picked my mother because she was attractive. I say this objectively—my father was less handsome than my mother was pretty. "Beauty and the beast," he'd say when he looked with us at old photographs. She'd protest, but there was some truth in what my father said, we all recognized this, especially my brother and I, who looked more like our father than we hoped to.

But my father would have understood that this was not a decision to be lightly taken. He would spend the rest of his life with this woman. He might have recognized, through whatever conversation he had with her, that this was someone who was his match, as acute as he was forgetful, as neat as he was messy. It's possible that this was evident at their meeting, but maybe not. Maybe they grew to complement each other later, my father realizing he could be dissolute with his memory because his wife would keep the trains running on time, my mother's temper growing moderate as my father's grew labile.

My dad was probably concerned with his household. He would have wanted a wife who could raise children and cook and clean. But then, none of the six women my father met would have failed in any of those criteria. My grandmother, his mother, would have seen to it that each of her potential daughters-in-law was capable of what she understood to be a wife's duties. I can't imagine my father differentiating more finely around that point.

The quality of that first interaction must have been deciding. Did she laugh when my father joked, did she make him laugh? Did she say something that struck him as being particularly keen or appropriate?

Inside the pizzeria, behind the counter, was another man, a friend of Frank's, whom my father did not recognize. The man was wearing a checkered jacket and a collared white shirt underneath. His age was unclear, because though my parents would eventually become skillful at differentiating gradations of that middle stretch of the lifespan, in 1969 my father was twenty-seven, my mother almost twenty-two, and all ages beyond forty—especially among Americans, who aged differently, it seemed, than Indians—were, to them, near indistinguishable. This older man waved hello and my parents waved hello back and sat down at a table.

My mother did not, that first time at the restaurant, register much about the place. She did not notice the fake-wood-looking wallpaper, the neon pink cursive in the window naming the place, the bathrooms in the back, one for men, one for women, the shared sink located in the hall between the two. She did not notice that there were three booths and six tables, that the booths could fit four, that the tables could fit two, that the tables were newer than the booths. She did not see that next door was a barbershop, could not have known that inside the shop was a table littered with magazines. These are things that came later, when, like a mapmaker, through a thousand small forays, she related in her head one place to the next in this, the New World.

Frank disappeared, then returned with two glasses of water. To my father he said, "Cheese, right?" and my father nodded. To my mother, Frank asked, "And what would you like to eat?"

My mother, unsure of her options, looked to her husband, who gestured to Frank and said in Gujarati, "Ask him what he can make for you."

But my mother, too uncertain with English to begin a conversation, said instead, "I will have what my husband is having."

"You like pizza?" asked Frank.

Searching for the right phrase, my mother said, "I think I will."

From behind the counter Frank's friend called out encouragingly, "That's the spirit."

When the pizza arrived, a small pie between the both of them, my father placed a slice onto my mother's plate and then another onto his own. My mother managed a bite or two. My father nudged, "It is good, yes?" and my mother nodded, though she thought the food miserable. It burned the roof of her mouth. The cheese stretched in cambers, long and languid, from her lips to the bit edge of the pizza and she could not, for the life of her, figure how to disconnect without using her left hand.

My father had begun to tell her about the first time he had eaten pizza when the stranger, Frank's friend, approached the table and said to my father, "Excuse me, son, would you mind if I helped your wife with her pizza?"

"Please," said my father, and the man they would, that next summer, when watching a televised basketball game, identify incredulously as Red Holtzmann, ruddy and cantankerous as his team loped across the Garden floor, pulled a chair alongside my mother and, laughing with her, explained that this was difficult food to eat. He showed her how to hold the slice by its crust, how to bend the slice almost in half, to let the tip droop slightly, so the oil would run off its surface, so that it would present itself easily to her mouth. He showed her to use her left hand to pull the stubborn mozzarella from her lips and when she had finished the slice, he left the table, patting her on the back, and said, "Young lady, you have a brilliant future in New York."

"Thank you," said my mother, and feeling more comfortable, she smiled at herself and with her husband.

"Now you are an expert," her husband said happily. "I should have shown you myself."

"We are both learning," said his wife, smiling broadly for just an instant.

I think this is what happened in February 1969. My father met with six women, all pretty, all smart, all capable of raising a family and managing a home. He sat and spoke with each of them, in the presence of their parents and his, over a cup of tea. There would have been nothing outrageous in the conversation, only a polite, lukewarm exchange. During the conversation, and in the hours afterward, my father would dwell on what was said, trying to intimate the young women's inner workings. He'd picture his wife in America, talking to Americans, learning with him a new way of living, because, I think, my father wanted a bride that he could share this new country of his with, someone who would marvel at the place with the same affection he did. And in my mom, perhaps, he sensed the edginess of a dream deferred. She couldn't be a doctor, she understood that her marks weren't good enough, but she still wanted a glimpse of a larger world, and something in her speech or her dress or her look conveyed that to him in their first meeting.

In choosing her, he was choosing a good Indian wife. Above all, my mother was that; her views, her tastes, her points of orientation not so different from those of her siblings in India, or heroines in Hindi films. But he was also choosing a fellow immigrant, someone who could navigate in his new home without pining the whole while for her old haunts, someone to whom he could whisper, "Look at that," and expect that she was seeing the same thing he was through the same appreciative eyes. Which is to say, my father chose his wife after he'd chosen his country.

iii.

On Tuesday it began to rain early in the morning, the sound a reliable monotone made, somehow, by a billion random collisions. The sky wavered between dark and darker gray overhead, and it turned to some compromise between the two out toward the horizon. My father's eldest brother was leaving for California, where the air was warmer and the sky more forgiving, after two weeks at our house.

My uncle and I passed two accidents on the way to the airport. The automobiles in each had slid into the median divider, jettisoning debris and paint and side-view mirrors, coming to rest closely applied to the concrete that kept the rest of us safe from oncoming traffic; the cars seemed bled of their vitality by the rain, the color of puddles. We on the road to other places were made misers by the resulting traffic snarls, grudging when we let other automobiles into our lanes, snatching, to the time of windshield wipers, inches and feet in fitful accelerations, decelerations.

We reached Kennedy at five-fifteen. My uncle's flight was at six. I helped him check in. He said mumbled kind words and I thanked him. Then he left, boarding pass in hand, to walk to his gate.

❄

I had taken a leave from school. I had nothing to do
at home. This is why I had time on my hands and why,
after watching my uncle pass through security, I wan-
dered about the terminal. In the bookstore, I thought to
buy a book but didn't. I thumbed through the *Atlantic*,
glancing every few paragraphs surreptitiously at the
covers of the adult magazines high on the back shelf,
hidden for the most part by *Field & Stream*, or else *Home*,
by the respectable sorts of magazines people ought to
be drawn to after their fathers have died.

I crept into a first-class lounge, just to see what it was
like, but a pretty and fragile blonde, icy in her airline
uniform, noticed my skulking. She asked to see my
ticket and then asked me to leave. At a gift shop I
bought Toblerone for my mother and my brother.

Later, feeling hungry, I bought myself a burger, fries,
and a Coke for nine dollars at an airport cafeteria. The
tables were crowded and I stood with my tray, rotating
in a circle, looking for an empty seat. I had turned
round three times when a seated Indian man, five tables
away, pointed to the chair opposite him.

"Please," he said, gesturing to the seat.

"Thank you."

The man was short and round, in his early thirties,
eating onion rings and sipping from a can of Coke. His
mustache was neatly trimmed, his bald spot smallish,
his glasses a thin, gold-colored metal frame. He was

wearing an exuberantly patterned polyester shirt rolled back from his wrists to just below his elbows. It matched, just barely, his ironed beige pants.

As I sat down, he said, with a newer immigrant's accent, "I brought this Coke from my home. If you buy the same Coke here, they'll take two dollars from you. If I bring it from home, it costs me ten cents."

"That's smart of you," I said, feeling the rube.

"Smart, nothing" said the man. "The smart people are the ones selling. In an airport people will spend anything."

"You may be right," I agreed.

"Maybe, nothing. De*fin*itely, I'm telling you. I'm in business myself. De*fin*itely." He leaned toward me over the table and motioned to the terminal surrounding with his arms, short and plump. "People are thinking one of two things in the airport. They are thinking, I am traveling, taking this trip, spending so much money, so what if I lose another ten or fifteen dollars? Or they are cursing themselves, because they do care about the money, but they are stuck in the airport and their car is parked in the parking lot. Where is your car?"

"In the lot," I said, on my way to proving his point.

"Of course. Now you are hungry. What to do, go walk to your car, drive twenty minutes there and back to get some food or some item?" He waited till I shook my head. "Not at all. People will grumble and people will mumble, but they will spend the money. In either case, if you are selling, you come out ahead. Your name, please."

"Rajiv Kothari," I said.

"Ajit Joshi," he replied, extending his hand.

Ajit was from Chandigarh, the best-planned city, he assured me, in all of India. He lived in Jackson Heights and worked at Sam & Raj, the electronics store. When he asked my line, I explained I was a medical student, and he beamed. "Very good," he said. "It is the best profession to be. My children will be doctors also."

"How many children do you have?" I asked.

"None yet."

Ajit looked at his watch. He had finished his onion rings and wiped his hands on a napkin. "Thirty minutes till our flight arrives," he said, inferring that we must be waiting for the same plane. "You know, my wife is coming today."

"Congratulations."

"Thank you," he said, smiling.

"How long have you been married?"

"More than three years now. She has stayed with my parents." He shook his head in a side-to-side wag. "We didn't think it would take this long. I spoke to an immigration lawyer and he told me ten months, *max*imum."

"You've seen her since the marriage?"

"I flew home three months ago, for her visa interview."

"You must be very happy," I said to Ajit.

"Like I cannot describe."

❈

My family, too, their applications sponsored by my father, had waited to come to America. In this, they were not unusual. Often years after they had first requested permission to emigrate, applicants would be scheduled for an interview in Delhi or Mumbai or Chennai. Traveling from all over India, they'd assemble on the pavement outside the American embassy or consulate, in the still-dark morning, and fight not to lose their places in line. Three hours later, when the building opened for business, the applicants passed through a security check and into a waiting room, with its industrial-strength floors, its fluorescent lights and molded plastic seats. There they'd sit, nervous and edgy in their new clothes and their newer haircuts, rehearsing their smiles and handshakes, reviewing silently, in tones of sincerity and practiced English, answers to the questions they anticipated.

Visa officers, minor American bureaucrats, were feared generally through the populace of hopeful travelers. After fifteen minutes of conversation the applicants were either approved or rejected, both instances sending the person to the nearest long-distance-dialing booth, to call home in either triumph or defeat, watching while they talked the meter that ticked away and measured their rupee charges in bright, digital red.

"Honestly, though, I tell you, I am a bit nervous about this business," Ajit said, his voice low and conspiratorial. "Our life will be difficult for her. At home she has a *dhobi* for the clothes and another woman comes to sweep and clean. Here, we have nothing. For three years she has been watching the American programs on Star television, to prepare. She thinks everyone in America lives so well." He looked again at his watch. "We should go now to wait for the plane. It will get so crowded soon. Pushing and shoving, just like India."

Arriving visitors, after completing examination at customs and immigration, passed into the receiving hall, where a clamor of persons waited, three deep to either side, behind metal railings. New arrivals walked slowly between the barriers, fumbling with baggage trolleys whose wheels seemed to jam diligently. They scanned faces, hoping to find one that looked familiar; they listened, hoping to hear their names called out. All around were other arrivals, and as they were recognized, they began to shout to whomever it was they knew and everyone else's job was made that much more difficult.

After thirty or so strides the path defined by the railings forked into left and right branches and the branches ended in a throng of hellos and hugs. People stopped at this bifurcation, sometimes for a desperate half minute, before, like a clarion or beacon, they heard a voice or saw a face, and knew they were safe.

This didn't happen to Ajit's wife. He stood, wedged between two larger people, against the rail, beside the entrance from customs. He'd wet and combed his hair. He was standing as straight and tall as he could manage. His wife, beautiful in an indigo sari, was one of the first through the doors and Ajit whooped her name, "OOOmaaa." She turned to him. She waved. He pointed her forward and walked parallel to the railing, behind the crowd, his head bobbing, sometimes visible, calling to her the whole way. I lost sight of the both of them.

I stood where I was for forty minutes, till all the passengers from India had left the receiving area, and two flights, one from Switzerland and the other from Russia, arrived and their passengers began to emerge simultaneously from immigration and customs.

When my father reached America, thirty-one years ago, he'd have disembarked from his plane, been interviewed by immigration, and passed through doors into some older reception hall. He'd have been more noticeable, though, one of a few Indians arriving.

The other Indians on the flight would have been almost exclusively young men, approximately his age. They would, like him, be heading to educational institutions, for graduate or postgraduate work. Most would be oriented toward the sciences: physicians, mathematicians, engineers. Their families would have come from a select subsection of the Indian population, if not exceedingly wealthy, enfranchised enough to afford some of the costs of travel and education.

When my father walked through the doors, a third cousin, already in the country, whom he hadn't seen since he was twelve, met him at the airport. This cousin's face would have been striking, one of a few Indian faces among the many more which blended into some generally white visage.

This evening the airport's receiving hall was flush with subcontinental mugs. There were more men than women, but enough women that a person wouldn't notice a disproportion unless he sat for forty minutes, counting and figuring as he watched. Though some people seemed to be new to the process, many more seemed practiced in moving over oceans and between continents. Entire families arrived after vacationing with relatives in India. Grandparents navigated the crowd familiarly, on their second or third trip abroad, meeting their children and their children's children.

My father would have had a more spacious amazement at his surroundings. The country would have been more distant, less familiar than it is to newly arriving immigrants from India, who have come to anticipate the place through television, through photographs and letters, through phone conversations and e-mail, through a creeping Westernization in their own country.

I left my post at the railing and was walking toward the exit when a hand tapped my shoulder and a man's voice said, softly, *"Bhaisaab?"* I turned to the voice and the man repeated, *"Bhaisaab?* I require some assistance."

The man was my age, perhaps a year or two older or younger, thin and wiry, my height. He wore gray slacks and a plain white shirt. He had one suitcase and a bag slung over his shoulder. *"Bhaisaab?"*

My father was a distinctive-looking man. Like his father, he had eyes and ears that seemed, on third or fourth glance, a hint too large. His nose, too, was largish, but defined so sharply that the impression it gave was one of decision, not oafishness. When he was younger, his face had been drawn but by the time he had died, the weight he'd gained had softened his face. His forehead was unremarkable, except when he would frown and it would furrow into haphazard creases, an irregularly tilled field.

The second man I met at the airport that day had none of these features. But he had my father's name, Vasant. He was starting a master's program in engineering at the New Jersey Institute of Technology, once the Newark College of Engineering, and he needed a ride.

Dear Father and Mother, dear Chotuji, dear brothers and sisters, dear nieces and nephews,

Jai Shri Krishna!

I am in America, at Suresh's flat in New Jersey, and my long flight is over. I wish I need never travel by air again. Lifting from the ground was itself a marvel. Though my seat was not near a window, I was able to sense our motion. The feeling was at first something like a train leaving the station. As we rose, however, I was pushed down into my seat, not simply backward, and it was as a person feels as a lift starts to move, only much faster. Later the plane leveled and it seemed my trip would be pleasant enough. But then our flight became violent, and I felt as though I were being thrown up and down and then from left to right. I began to think I might become sick.

For some time it seemed the feeling would pass, but the plane began to pitch and I experienced more strongly the need to vomit. I rose to go to the bathroom, so that no one else would be disturbed by my illness, but the room was occupied. I waited and waited, feeling my stomach as it turned and tumbled. When finally the occupant emerged from the bathroom, I was nearly lost. Narrowly avoiding the man, but missing also the toilet, I vomited. The bathroom in the airplane is very small and the last meal I had eaten in India covered it quite thoroughly.

I was forced to clean my mess while the plane was making it difficult simply to stand straight. When I returned to my seat, I realized I had made my new suit dirty as well, staining my right sleeve. Four times more during the flight I vomited, but during each of these instances I was able to reach the bathroom quickly.

Almost all the Indians who had boarded at Bombay disembarked in London and so Suresh found me at the airport without great difficulty — this though he approached first the fellow with whom I passed through immigration. That man was Gujarati also and as we were walking from the plane we found ourselves next to each other and began to talk. He is going to study medicine here. We collected our luggage together and passed through customs and immigration. He had forgotten his chest X ray in Bombay so I went before him, showed my own, without any suggestion of tuberculosis, and the official did not ask for his.

As it was, Suresh thought the doctor was me and introduced himself. The doctor redirected him and then Suresh and I waited until that doctor found the doctor who had come to meet him. We exchanged addresses and I hope to be in contact.

What to say about the American winter? How to describe the cold except to say that it hurts like a burn? As we walked to Suresh's car, frozen rain fell down upon us and it felt as though needles were stabbing at your skin. I don't know how a person can survive in a place like this. I sat in the car shivering and cursing. Suresh slapped my back and the cold made even that contact painful. He said, "Welcome to America." He asked me, "Do you have anything warm to wear in these two bags of yours?" I said, "I am wearing my warm clothing." He laughed like I was a clown and I laughed with him, though more from desperation than from amusement

It took us two hours to reach his house. You should see the roads here. They are as quiet and organized as lines on a sheet of paper. If it were possible, I would rather drive to America than fly to it. Suresh's flat itself is very nice. It has a drawing room, a kitchen, a bathroom and a bedroom. He shares it with two other students, one from Pune, one from near Madras. They fed me something and Suresh apologized for the food. "It is impossible to get the right ingredients here," he said. When I saw Suresh at the airport, I thought that he looked much thinner than he had in the photograph of him I had seen at home. Tasting the food here, I understand why.

Suresh, Naveen (from outside Madras), Rohit (from Pune), and I stayed awake until late into the night. They are all engineering students. I asked many questions about how to interact with Americans. They asked me question after question about news from India. They were hungry for even the smallest details. It was late at night when finally we slept.

I woke first the next morning, just as the sun was rising, and I took Suresh's keys from where he had left them on the table and put on his heavy overcoat. I went outside. I had seen from the window in the flat that the earth had been covered by snow. Even still, I could not anticipate the feeling of being in it. When I went to pick up the snow, it was light. When I pressed it between my hands, it became firm. When it began to melt into water I ate and drank it. It was so cold that my throat made a knot around it and I felt the knot until the water passed into my belly. I stayed outside for some time, experimenting with the substance.

When I went to return to the flat, my fingers could not put the key into the lock. I tried for minutes but my fingers did not feel familiar. Finally, someone leaving the building opened the door and let me in. I had the same problem at Suresh's door, but

I knocked and the locks were undone. My body has only now returned to me, after almost forty minutes and some pain, and so I am writing you. Both Suresh and his friends are now awake, preparing breakfast. I will ask Suresh to post this letter today so that you may all know what I have been doing.

With love and regards,

Vasant

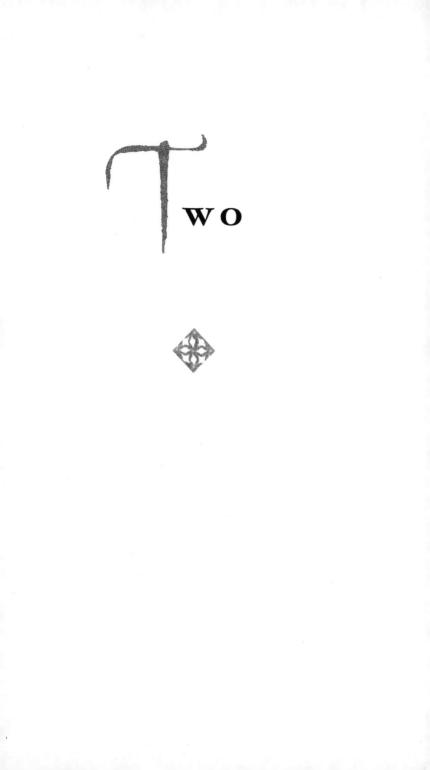

Two

It had been more than twelve years since I'd last been in India, just over three weeks since I'd met Vasant, when I stepped from the train I'd boarded in Bombay the night before onto a sporadically canopied railway platform in Gujarat. When the on-again, off-again corrugated-tin roofing admitted the midafternoon sun, it did so in broad and full slants, and the platform beneath, busy with dark faces and bodies, it made into a fluid and shifting mottle of light and shade.

In this rush, I caught sight of my grandfather almost immediately. My grandfather's frame, small and thin, was covered in a white cotton kurta pajama. His once speckled hair had turned a stern white and the change had made the lines of his face, brown framed now by white instead of black, clearer and more obvious. His cheekbones were prominent like elbows, his chin was square, and even his nose, still blunt at its tip and broad along its length, seemed somehow sharper. The round frames of his glasses ought to have softened his aspect, but in matching the curves of his eyebrows, their effect was one of studied and fastidious accessory. He looked, standing still as the platform seethed, as though the choice to age had been his alone, as if he had essentialized his person, sloughing off an old look for a new one that fit him better.

I shouted his name and he followed the sound tentatively till he saw me. He embraced me and pulled my forehead down to kiss it. He smiled widely. I smiled back. Again, he embraced me and kissed me. "Welcome home."

My grandfather's arm was wrapped around my shoulder as we walked. Behind us, an aged coolie balanced my two bags upon a piece of wrapped red cloth he had placed on top of his head. He followed us to the parking lot and loaded the luggage into the car my grandfather had hired. Our taxi, the color of cream, textured with dust, swelled in the anxious curves of an overdue pregnancy, the lines of its frame a throwback to a time some forty years past in the States, a car from a Dick Tracy comic book. The Ambassador was modeled after the British Motor Corporation's Morris Oxford, originally produced in 1948, copied by Hindustan Motors in 1950. Though a series of cosmetic modifications had been made to the automobile through the five ensuing decades, even the latest model years were flamboyantly antiquated and this persistent renewal, year after year, the continued production of that same, mid-century form—after the rest of the world had long since moved on to cars smaller and sleeker, more efficient, more reliable—had rendered the immigrant car indigenous. Even after Japanese and American and Korean and German cars made their way into the Indian market, offering higher standards of quality and convenience, the president of India plied the subcontinent's roads in new Ambassadors.

Shuddering as it started, shaking with every pause, the Ambassador kept its driver busy, pulling the choke or shifting gears. A rush of life, barely familiar, pressed against the car as we left the station. Through this life — bicycles and mopeds, motorcycles and ox carts, camels and vendors, men and women and children — the Ambassador asserted itself on the road in the way a rogue elephant might lord over a stretch of grassland, loudly, its horn blaring, its bulk demanding a path and accommodation.

"You chose a good time to visit us," my grandfather said. "This winter weather is pleasant." He nodded, agreeing with himself. "In the summer the air beats on you. Even sleeping is too much of an effort." He looked at me. "Can you imagine? You wake even more tired than you fell asleep. It is a downward spiral, pillar to post. See?" He made a face, tired and sleepy, mischievous, a child's parody. "Like this we meet the day. Small wonder we need tea."

It was a joke and I laughed. He laughed with me.

"I think we will have a good time here together, the two of us," said my grandfather.

❈

The taxi slowed. A bullock cart loaded with burlap sacks had eased onto the road. The bulls were gray and thin, their ribs almost clear beneath their hides. The driver fumed, his henna-colored mustache twitching in the rearview mirror like a caterpillar on fire.

My grandfather asked, "Tell me, doctor*ji*, why do people get heart attacks?"

I made a fist, a makeshift heart, and I held the heart between us. "The heart pumps blood to the whole body, but also to itself." My other hand traced imaginary arteries onto the fist; I clogged these with words. "When it can no longer pump blood to itself, when the path of the blood is blocked, the heart begins to die. The blockage was made over many years, by bad food habits, too much fat and oil, too much cholesterol, by not enough exercise."

My grandfather shook his head. "Incorrect, *beta*. You get a heart attack when your heart is broken."

"Stress can be a factor, also," I said, trying to agree with him.

"Then we are in accord," he said. "It was that place which killed him." The driver passed the ox cart. His mustache settled.

My grandfather is a storyteller. Thirteen years ago, when I was last in India, my extended family still lived with my grandfather and my grandmother in their house. The home was a modestly sized *haveli*, more than two hundred years old, just off a narrow street in the old part of town. From the street led a small alley that opened onto a small courtyard (every morning, someone from my family would place a bowl of peels and husks, the remnants of cooking from the day before, out onto its cobbled floor, and every morning, cows would make their way into the courtyard, eating the food and gracing us with their presence). Four doors led off the courtyard; the heavy and antique one on the right led to our home.

Though sprawling, the *haveli* was not large. Each nuclear unit of the extended family was given a room and the common spaces were shared. The younger children slept in the same rooms as their parents. The older children shared two rooms, one for the boys and one for the girls. The third floor was our rooftop and terrace, and when the weather made it uncomfortable to sleep inside, the whole family would climb the staircase and sleep under the sky in a long row of bodies, still warm, but cooler also.

Arranged in this fashion, his family prostrate beneath the night, my grandfather would begin his stories. The children listened most closely, but everyone paid attention and our parents would add details, filling out the narratives with parts they remembered from earlier versions. The stories, an admixture of history, religion, and myth, were purposeful, with lessons to learn and models of behavior to be mimicked or rejected. They were long or brief, though during the telling, I was unaware that time was passing. I always stayed awake till their ends and it was only afterward, after my grandfather had stopped talking, that seconds and minutes made sense again. Then, my mind racing, I'd wait forever till I fell asleep.

"Listen," my grandfather began as the taxi accelerated. "There once was a man who lived in a nearby village, a *sarkar*, you understand, a wealthy, powerful man." His voice had changed as it did on the roof years ago: low and heavy, projecting in a rumble, a lawyer's voice at summation, a preacher's voice in church, full of sureties and truths. Later, after I had stolen the car for him, I learned to be skeptical of his unsolicited offerings of wisdom. But when he began to speak, I caught his mood and then I sank into his voice because I knew the drill.

"He was wealthy, this *sarkar*, the wealthiest man in the village. He had many fields and the fields were always green. He started a business and the business was successful. He married a beautiful woman. She gave him a son, a strong and healthy boy. The man should have been pleased and content with everything he had, but was always concerned with how he might get more.

"This man had a servant, Ramu, who worked hard for him, day and night. In the early morning, before the sun rose, Ramu would wake and prepare tea and breakfast for the sarkar. He would light a fire, warming water for his master's bath. When his master left for his daily work, Ramu would clean the house till it was without a mark. When the sarkar came home, Ramu would attend to his every need. He would clean the kitchen when the cook had finished. Late at night, Ramu would stand outside his employer's bedroom door, to provide both him and his wife a glass of warm milk with almond mixed in before they slept. Then he would sing a song to send them both to sleep.

"Afterward, Ramu would leave the house, taking a thin sheet, and sleep on the packed earth outside. He would shiver when it was cold, he would sweat when it was warm, he would be bitten by insects the whole night long, but he would wake in the morning and dutifully begin his work again."

The taxi turned onto a smaller road. I scarcely noticed because the world had been made distant. "But Ramu was human and he had one great desire. He was becoming old. When he slept at night, his bones ached as they never had when he was younger. Insects seemed to feed on him more greedily and the packed earth seemed to be rockier. When he slept at night, Ramu would dream of the bed that the sarkar slept in. In his dream it would be the softest bed. It would take away all his pains and hurts.

"One evening, while the sarkar and his wife were in town attending a wedding, Ramu went to prepare their bed. This particular day had been very difficult for him. He ached more than he had ever ached before. He thought to himself, Sarkar-saab and mem-saab are away. I'll rest for only a few moments. Ramu lay down and immediately, he fell asleep.

"When his employer returned to find Ramu lying in his bed he was furious. He went outside and found a heavy branch. Returning to his room, he began to beat Ramu with a great and terrible passion."

My grandfather stopped and coughed. He watched my face as he finished and his hand delivered imaginary strikes. "With the first blow, Ramu awoke, confused. With the second blow he understood that he had fallen asleep and had been caught. With the third, fourth, and fifth blows, Ramu cried aloud and begged for forgiveness. With the sixth blow came a thought, and by the seventh blow that thought had become a realization. Ramu began to laugh and his master responded by becoming more angry, hitting harder and harder. Still Ramu laughed and finally the sarkar stopped his assault and demanded to know why his servant was laughing.

"Ramu said, 'I thought that sleeping in this bed of yours would ease my pain. But I am in greater pain than I was before. When I looked at you, beating me with such anger, a thought occurred to me. If this is the pain that comes with sleeping in this bed for just a few minutes, what pain you must feel, sleeping in it for hours, night after night, your months become years.'

"Think on this, Raju," said my grandfather. "It was that country that killed your father."

❖

The car made three turns, left, left, then right, into a series of progressively narrowing streets. After making its fourth turn, the car slowed and stopped. It could go no farther, the street a gulch too narrow for an animal of its size.

The house I had remembered in India was intricate, with carvings along the walls and little nooks and secret spaces. As children, we would play hide-and-seek, the games so interminably long that my brother or I or my cousins would invariably quit searching before the game was concluded. The street the car had stopped along was unfamiliar. The house my grandfather led me to was squat concrete, a quarter of the size of the old place. A blue-green paint was chipping and falling from its walls. In front of its door, a steady trickle of gray water, mildly pungent, flowed unashamedly. My skin began to itch.

"We've taken two rooms in this one," said my grandfather.

"I like the color," I said, not knowing what to say.

He threw his arm around my shoulder again, announcing to the fetid space, "We are agreed. A more beautiful color, I have never seen."

ii.

I called my grandfather Bapuji and my grandmother Ba.

Ba and Bapuji began to disagree almost immediately.

Bapuji and I climbed narrow and uneven stairs and entered through an unlatched door into one of the apartment's two rooms. Its concrete walls, painted bright blue, were bare except for two portraits of my grandfather's parents, their faces framed in black-stained wood, safe under dusty plates of glass. The pictures were garlanded and hung opposite the door that had opened onto the stairwell, five and a half feet above the ground, heads without bodies. To the left and right of the portraits were two doors painted in a thick and running brown which led to the kitchen and bathroom, respectively. Above our heads, a lazy fan, colored by the same syrupy paint, offered the hint of a breeze. A narrow bed was pushed into a corner, a small desk and chair next to it.

Ba emerged from the kitchen in a rush of motion, the white sari that covered her stout frame billowing like a sail. Seeing me, she stopped, and began to laugh and cry. Clapping her hands, she called in a singsong voice, "My child has come home, my child has come home, my child has come home." Then, regaining momentum, she lavished me with a tight and sustained hug. My grandmother's face was as round and full as a fresh teardrop. There was not a landmark on my father's face that had suggested his mother. But his expressions and his smiles, the way he had demonstrated happiness — these were Ba's.

Bapuji, standing at the top of the stairs, ended Ba's embrace, calling into the room, "Hug him later, there is time for that. I need some money to pay the taxi."

My grandmother released me. "How much was the taxi?"

"Three-ninety," Bapuji said.

Ba sagged, her sari growing new wrinkles and creases. She shook her head. "Too much. From here to the station and here again shouldn't be more than three hundred."

"There was luggage," said Bapuji after a moment.

"With luggage, I am saying."

"He's asking for three-ninety."

Ba stared at him. Bapuji shifted his weight and shifted it back again.

"I'll go talk to the driver," she said finally and, gathering her sari around her, began to walk toward the door.

"No need for that," Bapuji said. Shaking his head, to me he said, teasing, "We can't have your Ba scolding the driver. The poor man won't get a single paisa." Then, again to Ba he said, "Give me three hundred. I'll see if he'll take it."

"Of course he'll take it," she said. "Even that is too much."

She walked into the kitchen and emerged with a small stack of ten-rupee notes. She gave these to my grandfather, who disappeared down the stairs. When he had gone, with my father's frown on her face, she said to me quietly, "Your grandfather has become a cheat with money. He'll give the driver two hundred sixty and keep forty for himself." Then, "Go, he'll need help with the luggage."

Outside, the driver had unloaded the bags and left. Seeing me, Bapuji announced pleasantly, "He took the money. It's not like your country, with plastic tags and computer codes. In our Hindustan, everything is negotiable."

Ba had cooked for us. Bapuji and I sat on the floor of the room that opened onto the staircase, Ba's room. We ate while Ba served us, our *thalis* full with *daal* and *baath, subzi* and *roti.* When I thought I had finished, she insisted that I eat a sweet, a *ladoo,* wheat flour soaked in butter and sugar syrup. Then another and another, dropping them into my *thali* till I remembered the appropriate gesture and held my hands, my fingers spread, my palms facing down, over my empty dish. Ba relented.

My grandfather said, with a hint of pride in his voice, "When I was your age, I would eat twelve or thirteen of those after I had finished my meal."

Ba and I looked at each other, each imagining my

grandfather, five feet tall, thin as a rail, eating a dozen *ladoos*. Ba puffed her cheeks out, making a face, and said, "Then he wouldn't move the whole day, trying to hold everything in."

He glared at her and without the same humor in his voice, said, "What would you know of it?"

My grandmother cleared the plates.

"You must be wanting a bath?" Bapuji asked. We had moved into the back room, the smaller of the two — Bapuji's room — while my grandmother ate in the other. The room was ten by eight. Along the wall it shared with the larger room was a row of shelves stacked with clothes and books. Another wall opened onto a small balcony that overlooked the street. The bed, a wood and rope frame on which rested a stuffed cotton mattress, was wedged into a corner.

"I'd love a bath," I said.

"Take a bath and then have a nap. You must be tired." He walked into the main room, where Ba was seated, eating her lunch, and unbolted the brown door to the bathroom. About to enter, he paused to ask, "Do you want hot water?"

"If that's possible."

"Why not?" he said. "Everything is possible."

He returned to his room and rummaged slowly under his bed till he found a long coil of gray metal attached to a black plastic casing, the casing connected to a long electric cord. He slung the device around his shoulders.

I entered the bathroom with him. It was gray cement

throughout, with a small half window that admitted a vague and indirect light from outside. A splintering wooden shelf, just below the window, bore a bar of soap. In one corner was a keyhole-shaped toilet flush with the floor. Next to the toilet was a spigot. Another spigot was in the opposite corner of the room, beside the door. Bapuji turned it open, letting the water run and clear before catching it in a large, red plastic bucket. When the bucket was near full, he dragged it to the center of the room. He found an outlet along the wall and into this he plugged the heating coil. He looped the cord once and, stretching on his toes, hung the loop from a hook secured in the low ceiling. From the hook the coil dangled, six inches above the ground, swinging back and forth above the floor. Bapuji dragged the bucket of water to the coil, placed the coil in it, and repositioned the bucket once again. Immersed in the water, swaying slightly, the coil began to warm water for my bath.

"See," said Bapuji, satisfied and winded, "everything is possible."

I finished my bucket bath, dressed, and emerged from the bathroom. Bapuji had fallen asleep, taking his afternoon nap in the back room. His snoring, gentle and barely obtrusive, dusted the apartment, and was marked now and again by the conversation of birds perched on the balcony.

I almost saw the sun rise my second morning in India. After bathing, I'd slept through the afternoon and the evening and into the night on matting Ba had unrolled for me on the floor of her room. Resting at the wrong times, I compensated by waking at the wrong times also, so that at three in the morning I was up and the city was asleep. A glow from the night touched the inner room lightly, and by concentrating, I could see the darkness of my hand against the darkness of the air.

I passed hours awake, my eyes closed, my eyes open, and the silhouette of my spread fingers passed from black to gray. Creeping to the balcony off Bapuji's bedroom, I looked out and could only see the building opposite and the street below, the horizon and the sun lost to me. But above the sky reddened and lightened and in this way I measured the day's start.

It was not a quiet dawn. A fat milkman rode by on a skinny bicycle. The bicycle squeaked and rattled. Two steel containers heavy with milk balanced on either side of the cycle and with each dip and bump in the sometimes paved, sometimes unpaved road, they would shift with a clatter and a clang. The milkman rang the bicycle's bell to warn sleeping dogs and all others that needed to know that they had better move, because like a tightrope walker, his path was set. The ring of the bell bounced briefly off the buildings that crowded the street before burrowing into the earth and evaporating into the sky. Dogs barked in reply, and these sounds, too, echoed before they retreated.

Pairs and groups of women dressed in brightly colored cotton saris made their way along the street. Household help, they were, laughing and talking, owners of the hour. Their skin was dark and nutty, a color closer to the night now past than the day, newly beginning.

My grandfather woke. He reached for the glasses he kept on a small metal table beside his bed. Fitting them, eyes focusing, he saw me on the balcony. "Awake already?" He coughed once and then again. "Good. I wake at this time as well. Your grandmother must be awake also."

I looked into the other room. Ba was no longer in her bed. The light in the kitchen was on. Quiet noises came from inside. There was a soft burst of air as she ignited the burner that subdued when she reduced the flow of gas.

"Is she making tea?" I asked.

Bapuji shook his head in the side-to-side way that meant yes.

"Does she need help?" I asked.

Bapuji shook his head in the side-to-side way that meant no.

The last time I had been in India, the kitchen, in the old house, had been populated. My grandmother, my aunts, my female cousins, my male cousin's wives, would all pass in and out of the room. My mother, too, on arriving in India, would separate from my father, clustering with the other women in and around the kitchen. My father would sit with the men in the largest room of the house, dressed in white cottons that he rarely wore in America.

It had seemed, then, a social and festive separation. That first morning, the pageant made spartan, reduced to my grandmother and grandfather, it seemed that husband and wife were caught in orbit around two different stars, an expanse of empty space between them.

We drank our tea together, seated on the floor in Ba's room. The tea came in small, neat ceramic cups placed on saucers. We poured the tea out of the cups into our saucers, balancing the saucers above our palms on the five fingers of our right hands. The tea steamed and cooled. We blew gently on the liquid before we sipped.

Outside, the street grew nosier, full with shouts and people. Bapuji looked at Ba. She rose, walked into his room, and drew heavy wooden shutters over the windows that opened onto the street. The place was quieter and dimmer and Bapuji seemed pleased by the change.

iii.

Bapuji and I went for a walk after the tea. The lane outside his house was mostly pressed dirt. It connected to a larger, paved street. That street, eight feet wide, was a place of transit as well as commerce. It accommodated movement only centrally; two feet on either side were stationary. This space was reserved for transactions, economic and social, between shop owners, whose stores opened without a wall intervening to positions raised slightly above the street, and passersby.

The house I remembered in India was along a busy street also. That street had been my grandfather's own. Merchants would shout greetings to him. From overlooking apartments, families would call out. Because Bapuji knew them all, he navigated the street laboriously, along its edges, stopping to speak with each person who'd announced his name. The simplest of errands took time.

When, thirteen years ago, my father had asked his father to move to America, Bapuji led his son to one of the many balconies in the old house, a wood and stone perch above the street. They sat there an hour, drinking tea and eating biscuits. In that time six people stopped to speak with Bapuji, all six recognizing my father as well. The argument concluded in this way, my grandfather left his son to sit looking out over a lane that remembered him still.

This morning we moved quickly, in the center of the street, with what felt like purpose.

"So where are we going?" I asked my grandfather some minutes into our motion.

"We are just walking," he said amiably. "Do you want to go somewhere?"

"No," I answered, somewhat surprised. "Just walking is fine with me."

The morning was consumed in strides. Bapuji's apartment was in the old town. Perhaps two miles square, the entire area was of a similar age. It was clear, however, that some parts had fared more poorly than others. Near Bapuji's house, the streets were cluttered with refuse and debris. Pigs rooted through this urban flotsam not unlike vultures around a carcass, at ease but also alert, ready to flee at the suggestion of any motion not their own.

Though sewer lines ran under the streets, less offensive waste water, from sinks and the like, ran, discolored, above the ground in open gutters. The liquid smelled musty and fertile, though not so in the middle of the streets. Rather, it was only when a person paused at the entrance to a house, waiting for a door to open, that the scent rose slowly to his nose, where it settled, humid and full.

Beyond my grandfather's neighborhood was another, equally aged. Somewhere in this adjoining quarter had been his old home. While the streets here were also narrow, they were clean. All drainage was hidden from view. The houses, made of the same roughly hewn stone and concrete, had brightly painted doorways and windows. They seemed less in decline. Things porcine were replaced by things bovine, grander and less furtive. The space around Bapuji's apartment felt crudely medieval; passing through this bordering locale made one feel that there might have been a time when the whole of the old city was exquisite, fine.

We turned from one street to the next, sometimes emerging onto wider main roads, most of the time pressed against each other in narrow alleys. Despite differences in size and traffic, most streets were variations on a theme, cobbled or paved, bordered by stores. Above the stores sat squat apartments and homes. Individual buildings shared two side walls with their neighbors, and this connected structure continued, its facade and height and breadth changing from building to building, until one alley was stopped by another. At these junctions there was a pause in the matrix and after a rest of space, a new ramble would begin.

Similarly structured alleys were made distinguishable by their shops. Along one lane stores would sell rubber tires; along another gold stores clustered, protected by security guards and the ugly, heavy rifles they carried. There was an alley with nothing but saris and there was a gully with nothing but furniture makers. The shops identified themselves with long, thin, tin signs. Lettered in English and Gujarati, the signs were bravely colored, in sky blue, or blood red, or sunset orange, and though a shop might seem desolate, its proprietor lonely, in need of customers, its sign would be majestic. It was in the midst of these plots of commerce that I began to think of nothing, feeling content to stroll a step behind my grandfather, my feet and eyes and ears alive in the mazy moment.

"Are you tired?" my eighty-one-year-old grandfather asked after almost an hour of walking.

"I'm fine. How are you doing?"

"One hundred and one percent fine."

"Are you certain?"

"Ninety-nine percent sure."

"Let's rest for a while," I said.

We walked another thirty feet to stand on the street governed by a wiry man with a wiry mustache. He was dressed in a slightly dirty, wide-collared, white, half-sleeve shirt and tight gray pants.

"Do you like *paan?*" my grandfather asked me.

"I might."

"With tobacco or without?"

I hesitated.

"Then you take it without," Bapuji said.

He ordered a *mitaü paan,* a Fanta, and a Limca.

The man handed us our sodas. We wiped clean the

mouths of the opened glass bottles and began to drink.

The vendor prepared the paan. He took a leaf the size of his palm from a bowl in which it had been soaking, and, after tearing its edges to perfect its size, lay the leaf flat on the wooden surface of his stand. Around the leaf were sixteen or seventeen small stainless-steel canisters. These the man opened and then capped in a controlled burst of movement, removing, in the process, some ingredient he would drop or flick or daub onto the leaf. After opening and closing some select series of the canisters, the man folded the leaf three times, once in half and then twice more, back onto itself, so that when he was done it was a tightly fashioned triangle, glistening green all around. Inside my mouth, it was sweet and light, the competing textures cool on my tongue.

Bapuji and I leaned against a scooter parked on the side of the road, sipping our sodas. I finished first and returned my bottle to the vendor, who placed it in a blue plastic crate with the others that would be cleaned and refilled. Bapuji did the same. I burped then he burped and we looked at each other, satiated.

Facing the vendor, his back to me, Bapuji reached into his white cotton trousers. His hand had settled firmly into the pocket before his body froze. Nervous, he turned round to me.

"Raju, have you any money? I've forgotten my own. Do you have any rupees or just dollars?"

I nodded. "I changed some money at the airport."

I found a hundred-rupee note. I showed it to him. The vendor intervened, demanding smaller change. Returning the bill to my wallet, I found fifty. I gave it to the vendor. Again he asked me for a smaller note. I told him I had none. Grumbling, he found thirty-three rupees' change, which my grandfather collected in his outstretched hand and deposited into his pocket.

Dear Father and Mother, dear Chotuji, dear brothers and sisters, dear nieces and nephews,

Jai Shri Krishna!

I am waiting for your letters. They have not yet come, but I am sure they are in transit. My new address is on this envelope and you no longer need send my mail via the college. I now share a flat with a good-natured Jain whose father is in the textile business in Ahmedabad. Both of us are studying electrical engineering.

I am teaching first-year students in the laboratory and today was our inaugural experiment. We began by taking a small, shallow circular dish, not more than four inches across. We filled the dish with water. Then we dropped drops of oil onto the dish until a layer covered the water. By counting the number of drops and utilizing some information on the structure and weight of oil molecules, the students were to calculate the thickness of the layer of oil on top of the water.

Feeling anxious, I had prepared this first experiment the whole week through. I wrote answers to questions I supposed they might ask prior to the session, so that grammar would not be a problem, and I practiced the night before with a neighbor of mine. I was wearing the tie Father had bought me before I left and a white lab coat provided by the university.

The students, all boys except for one girl, were initially respectful. When I took attendance, there was some laughter as I mispronounced names. I smiled with them at first as I did not want to be an unfriendly teacher. I started my lecture. After two minutes, one boy asked me what we were to put in the glass dishes. This was a very basic point. I thought I had explained it very clearly. I told him "Water" so he would not be so confused. The class began to giggle. I thought they were teasing the boy for having missed this very simple point. I felt badly for him. Immediately there was a second question, and another boy asked me, what was the oil to cover? I said again "Water." Again the class laughed. I began to worry that my students might not have understood me, so I quickly summarized the lecture. I asked if there were any questions. A third boy asked me again, what were we to put in the glass dishes first? "Water."

The class was laughing so hard some of them were tearing. Only one boy and the girl were quiet. They both looked embarrassed. I finished my talk and set everyone to work. During the laboratory almost half of the students asked me a question that had "water" in the answer. It is because we do not have a letter w and so my pronunciation is incorrect. I try to say it like a v but with breath in it. This is what they found funny. Despite my preparation I was made a clown.

My roommate, Vijay, had the same difficulty. We share a laboratory space and he is in charge of fifteen students just as I am. His students heard my students and the ridicule was infectious. I thought to complain to him in Gujarati, but then felt the sound of our language in that room would make us both more vulnerable. This was the difficult part of the day and perhaps you are thinking that I am having only a difficult time in America but this country has wonders also.

When we had cleaned the lab and the sun had set, I walked home with Vijay. It began to rain. Neither of us had brought an umbrella. With more than a mile to walk, I did my best to shelter my books and my face. Vijay made no such effort. He was *dejected. He let his eyeglasses cover with raindrops and he almost fell.*

"Wipe your glasses, yaar," I told him.

He said, "No, sir. With my glasses covered with drops, I think this place looks like home."

The place we were walking did not look like Ahmedabad at all.

"How is that possible?" I asked him.

He said, "When it rains at home, I can't see a damn thing either."

So I turned my face to the sky and covered my glasses, too, with raindrops until I couldn't see anymore either. Vijay was correct. It began to look like home. I thought I might see you the next minute instead of the next year.

I tripped twice before we had reached the next street. A moment later, Vijay walked into a dustbin along the road. I began to laugh very hard. I wiped my glasses off and so did Vijay. Both of us stopped and looked at the town. Vijay said, "Where is it that we have come too?"

The roads here are all paved with black tar so that when it rains, they do not become sloppy with mud. Instead the pavement shines, like it has been polished. There are lights along poles that line the streets and brighten the city when it becomes dark. The road did not reflect this light, but it did not ignore it either. It held the glow like a child, cushioning it in the water of its puddles. As far as we could see, the lights were brilliant above and soft and wavering below. It is a beautiful thing to behold and I have never seen a thing like it before. This country was made for the taking of photographs. It is for this reason, perhaps, that America invented the camera.

My spirits began to lighten and I said, "This is Newark. Where did you think we were?"

Vijay caught the mood in my voice. Not to be left looking foolish, he said, "Newark? Newark? Arre! I asked them to send me to New York! I said, send me to New York, give me a big scholarship, arrange my housing for me, and, please, I am Jain, can you make some arrangement about the food? Had I only been in New York everything would have been taken care of."

"It's your damn foreigner accent. When you say 'New York' and 'Newark' it sounds like the same place."

My first American friend is the neighbor I mentioned earlier. Her name is Evelyn and she is an elderly Negro lady. Evelyn was walking out from our building with an umbrella as we were walking in. She scolded us for walking about in the rain and hurried us to our rooms. We changed into dry clothes. By the time we had done so, she returned to our apartment with tomato soup and toasted bread to eat. She asked how our lectures had been received.

Neither Vijay nor I wished to disappoint her because she had helped us so enthusiastically in our preparations. I told her the sessions had gone well and when she asked for particulars, Vijay told her that our students were intelligent and polite. I told her that the experiment itself went flawlessly and thanked her for her help. She said that it was no trouble at all.

Evelyn spoke about her children. When they were young, they each loved science. One daughter is married in Chicago and works as a nurse. Another daughter lives in Florida. Her son lives nearby in New York City. Her husband passed on three years ago. Vijay asked her why it was that she did not live with her son and she said, "Well, I don't want to be a bother to him.

And I know I don't want him to be a bother to me." I thought that there must be some difficulty between them, yet when she speaks of him, it is without bitterness. Vijay commented afterward that this sort of separation was typically American, but I am not certain I believe him. He has only been in the country a month longer than I.

Evelyn knows most people in the building and has introduced me to them all. Most are Negroes although there are a few Americans. My neighbors have named me "Little-man." Vijay is called "Big-Little-man." He does not like the name, but given his weight, I am inclined to agree that it is appropriate. However, because of our difficulty with food, it seems that this situation will change.

I have already grown tired of toast and jam. I eat fruits, too, but the bananas here are terrible. Most other food contains some type of meat. When I tell people that I do not eat meat, they offer chicken and fish. When I tell them I cannot eat these things either, they ask me, "Then what will you eat?" It is something worth wondering. I have started to eat large amounts of pizza, a food from the Italian people. It is bread covered with a spiced tomato paste and cheese. This is not to say that it is properly spiced, but it has its merits.

I suggested this food to Vijay and he agreed to come to the restaurant. He is, however, trying to keep a strict Jain diet. After I placed my order, Vijay tried to buy something for himself. The man selling the pizza asked if he also ate without meat. Vijay said, "Yes, no meat, no chicken, no fish. Also, please, nothing that was grown under the ground. No potato, no garlic, no onion, no carrot." The man selling the pizza began to laugh. Vijay looked as though he would weep. Finally the man made him a piece of pizza without the tomato sauce, just bread and cheese. Vijay would not have been more happy if he had been given a mango and a mitai.

So, my dear family, you see that it will take us both some time to adjust to this country. But be at ease and do not worry about us. We are better adjusted than we were only two weeks ago. We have a place to live, a neighbor who cares for us, and a place from which to purchase food. In a month, we may be able to say the word "water." When this happens, who is to say that we will not be proper Americans?

I am waiting to hear from you. I miss you all.
Deepest love and regards,

Vasant

Three

i.

Vasant was headed to Jersey. He'd expected to be received at the airport by an uncle. He searched the receiving hall three times and grew more desperate with each pass. He had no currency. He tried, but couldn't use, the telephone. In this state, feeling as if events were conspiring against him, he grabbed the shoulder of the most approachable brown face he saw and asked for help.

Vasant was dressed in a white shirt that had been visibly crumpled during his flight. His look was nondescript: an average-sized face, an unremarkable nose, a normal chin, distinct but not distinctive eyes, hair that parted neatly on the left. The sum effect of so much normalcy was disconcerting: there were no distinguishing features and I looked at his face like a man lost in a foreign country, for landmarks that weren't there.

Though he'd called to me in Hindi, we spoke to each other in English. He was comfortable with the language and while I'd understood his greeting, my difficulty with the tongue was obvious. He was Marwari. He had graduated from the Birla Institute of Technology at Pilani with a degree in electrical engineering. He was entering a master's program at NJIT when the January semester began. He explained this by way of introduction and, afterward, asked for assistance using the phone.

I helped him place a call. A cousin on the other end accepted the charges and passed the phone to her mother. His aunt explained to him that his uncle had had a small accident. He'd called home just before Vasant to relate that he'd slid off the road. Airbags had exploded, but the uncle was fine. He had gone to the hospital as a precaution. She was headed just now to collect him. Later she would come to get Vasant. Four or five hours, she said, no longer. They said good-byes. Vasant thanked me for my help and explained his situation.

"If it would make things easier for all of you," I suggested, though my home was in New York, though my mother was waiting for me, though my brother and I had plans to see a movie that night, "I am heading into New Jersey, too. I could give you a ride."

Vasant called back; again his cousin answered and accepted the charges. Vasant explained my offer to his aunt and passed the phone to me. I was on my way into northern Jersey, I told her, and it wouldn't be a problem to drop Vasant at her house. She hesitated until I gave her my name and explained I was in medical school. Then, giving directions, she thanked me for making her life easier. I passed the phone to Vasant. He exchanged a few more words with his aunt. He returned the phone to its cradle and waited.

"All right, then," I said. "Follow me."

❖

The rain had slowed to a drizzle and the day had passed into the early dark of a winter evening. The parking lot was evenly divided between people who had opened their umbrellas to keep dry and people to whom umbrellas were more of an inconvenience than water. From a spot overhead came the deceptive Doppler rumble of an ascending plane. In an altogether different place was the plane itself, lights blinking somewhere above the horizon and below the sky, a hundred, then a thousand feet high.

As we walked to the car I lied to Vasant, explaining I had been involved in some sort of mix-up, that the flight I thought was arriving today was in fact arriving tomorrow. "Well," he said affably, "thank you for your error. It is to my benefit." It occurred to me then, and then only briefly, that it was odd I was driving to New Jersey. I had a parochial aversion to the state, and in the way I disregarded the Dakotas, I disliked Jersey.

"How was your flight?" I was loading the trunk with his suitcase.

"You would not believe," said Vasant, reaching to help me. "The airline made a mistake and did not pack enough vegetarian meals. Then the women serving the food asked us if, since they were short of completely vegetarian meals, would a chicken meal do? After all, she said, it is not really meat. Well, the man to whom she said this started shouting and pointing to his family.

His wife and two baby girls were there. They were beautiful children. Do you want to corrupt them? he asked. What should the lady reply to that question?"

We laughed. The suitcase slid into place. "I'd be upset, too," I said, shutting the trunk.

"And then the crew suggested, well, could all the vegetarians take the meat meals, and have the rice and vegetables from them without eating the meat? Then I began to yell as well."

"You're vegetarian?"

"No, actually. But I was upset for everyone else. They fixed the problem in London. I think the crew must have phoned ahead with headaches because of these crazy vegetarians. There is nothing more frightening than hungry Indians," said Vasant. Then, smiling in disbelief, "Grandmothers were shaking their canes."

I paid for parking and Vasant lapsed into silence, staring out the window. We eased onto the Van Wyck, still slow. The cars had been polished from the grays of afternoon to sparkling, mostly stationary, columns of headlights and taillights, snaking to the city, snaking to the airport. Then the traffic eased and we accelerated.

"The weather is like this at this time?"

"It's generally colder."

"When is it snowing?"

"It already snowed some. It comes and goes through the winter."

"Comes and goes," he repeated.

❄

I am not at all certain why I offered Vasant a ride.

Before I left school my class had dissected cadavers to precise parts, table after the next, till one started to look like another. And though my classmates and I took pride in the chance particulars of our bodies, we were like neighbors in Levittown, differentiating by shades of lawn color and tints of aluminum siding houses which were the same. Bodies, all of them, were sensible. Vessels led to other vessels, big then small or otherwise smaller then bigger; muscles pulled on bones and attached to eyeballs in six places; nerves coursed diffusely through the body like a perfect electrical spiderweb. I enjoyed anatomy, that events had conspired so favorably, that the construction had been so precise. I did well in the class because I liked it, and I liked it because of the order and regularity.

Occasionally the muscles arranged themselves at bizarre angles, taking right turns, splitting, overlapping, running themselves through slings. Nerves turned back on themselves. Those nights, disoriented, I'd stay late in lab trying to find north. When I came home, my clothes and fingers thick with the aroma of formaldehyde, my head buzzed and I'd feel dizzy. I'd shower and force myself to read something innocuous till I felt better settled.

In retrospect, I think my mind was feeling a bit foreign well before I decided to steal the car for my grandfather. Why was I driving Vasant into New Jersey?

Because he had my father's name, because he was newly arrived from India, because he was going to my father's college: this is part of it, but not nearly all of it. I can only say that I was not feeling much like myself and I won't hazard a guess on the motivations of a person so unfamiliar.

It is easier, I think, to see why Vasant might have so quickly made me his friend. He'd been stranded and lost, then rescued. To the person who had rescued him, he afforded some license, some trust. Through circumstance and propinquity, I was his first new friend on this side of the world.

I turned on the radio and scanned through the stations. I heard an advertisement for Bayer aspirin, an advertisement for home refinancing, an advertisement for a morning radio show, a caller whose husband couldn't achieve an erection, disc jockeys yammering, a caller upset with the Knicks' substitution patterns, a plea for clean drinking water, a trumpet solo, soaring then settling quietly into the thrum of an upright base, a piece of classical music I would never recognize, pop and rock and rap songs familiar as family.

I turned toward Vasant and his eyes were closed. He was listening intently, imbibing. Then he opened his eyes. "I love this music," he said. After asking permission he adjusted the speakers, fading the noise from front to back, throwing the notes and tones from left to right and then right to left again. Cradling and containing this flux of sound, we passed into view of the New York skyline.

"Is that New York?"

"That's Manhattan."

"Will we pass through it?"

"We'll drive by it. We might get a little closer. I think you'll have a better view."

"Can you name the buildings?"

"Those two tall ones are the World Trade Center. The tall one in the middle with the red, white, and blue lights is the Empire State Building. The other tall one, almost next to the Empire State Building, is the Chrysler Building."

Vasant found each of the buildings. "I like the Chrysler Building," he decided.

"That is my father's favorite building. He knows everything about it."

"What sorts of things?"

"About the architecture. The building has these gargoyles—on most buildings they are shaped like monsters, but on the Chrysler, they're shaped like the parts of an automobile. I think they are shaped like the hubcaps. Hubcaps with wings."

"What else?" Vasant said and when I looked over to him he was staring at me. I turned from his gaze, back to the road.

"There is a story about the building during its construction. When it was almost finished it wasn't certain that it would be the tallest building in New York. There was another skyscraper that was just as tall, maybe even taller. But the owners had built a spire inside the Chrysler's top floors. No one knew about it. In a single day, in only ninety minutes, they hoisted the needle onto the top of the tower. For a few months it was the greatest building in the whole world."

"That is amazing," said Vasant.

"I know."

Then Vasant said, "Imagine those fellows in the belly of that building. Each day at the end of work they must have wanted to shout what it was they had hidden. They would have wanted to whisper their plans to their wives and their friends; they would want to brag to their children. But the whole while they had to keep their quiet, waiting, waiting, waiting." After a moment he asked, "What are the other buildings?"

"I don't know," I said.

He smiled. "In America, they are as common as trees."

"Is Chrysler the most popular car in America?"

"I think it's the Honda Accord. I'll show you if we pass one."

"And what are the different models available?"

"Of Accords?"

"Of cars in general."

"Oh," I said. "I don't know. There are a lot."

"I am noticing this."

"How about in India?"

"In India the most popular car is the Maruti."

"Does your family have one?"

"We have an Ambassador. It is a larger car, well suited to the Indian roads, but a bit old-fashioned. It was once the most popular car in India but since liberalization, there are many more cars to choose from. People are not buying the Ambassador so much anymore." Vasant smiled. "Perhaps if things go well for me in America, my family will be able to replace our car with a Mercedes."

ii.

Vasant was more comfortable in English than my father had been when he arrived from India. In those years after Independence it was taught without great conviction, as a third language, and even my grandfather, for whom command of the tongue was a job requirement, discouraged its use in favor of Hindi and Gujarati. In college, though the texts and lectures had been in English, outside class students conversed in Gujarati. Examinations required mostly mathematical calculation.

On arriving in the States, my father found his English lacking. He learned the language piecemeal, and though his command increased as the years passed, he was constantly made aware of the gaps. He'd come home having spent the day ruminating on a phrase and ask for a translation. "Six-of-one-half-a-dozen-of-another. What does that mean?"

His grammar was poor. He would add articles to his sentences: "I'm going to watch the play-offs with the Bob." Writing was especially difficult. In sixth grade, I began to proofread his correspondence. I'd help my cousins write résumés and letters of inquiry. My brother started helping when he was in fifth grade, because his English was particularly strong.

The language dulled my father's wit. The jokes he made seemed clumsy. He'd take too long to relate an anecdote. He'd choose words not in accord with the mood he was trying to create. He was uproarious in Gujarati. The same joke, told in English, was handicapped: too cumbersome, badly timed, unsteady. He appeared a sterner person, I think, to Americans than to his Indian immigrant peers.

My father grew frustrated when he had to repeat himself. He would be forced to say the same thing two or three times, each time adjusting his inflection, slowing his speech, enunciating, till whomever he was speaking to finally nodded in agreement. "Oh, you want the *Allen wrenches*. They're in aisle twelve," the person might reply, instructing with his answer. My father would feel this was his second month in the country instead of his twenty-fifth year.

I glanced at Vasant as he looked through the passenger window, out onto the dimly lit cuff of the New Jersey Turnpike. I wondered how he had looked when he was younger; I imagined the ways his face would change as he grew older. If life was kind to him, he might emerge on the other side of his next thirty years heavier and grayer but unscathed.

"Do you go back to India often?" Vasant asked me.

"I haven't been back since I was eleven."

"Most of your family is there?"

"They were when I went. Most of my family is here now."

"Did you like India?"

"Yes and no."

From the ages of seven to ten I had come to my sense of the subcontinent through comics, Indian, purchased singly from the city, or occasionally arriving from India packaged in a volume. I attached great value to these books. They became my earliest, most rudimentary form of currency. If I was good, for a week, for two weeks, if I committed no major transgression, I'd get one or two of these comics each month, and if my conduct was found wanting, I had to wait.

There was a single publisher of the books, Amar Chitra Katha, and its symbol, a black chakra on a small yellow square, would appear in the upper left corner of each cover, along with an issue number. The pages were unglossed and rough, but the colors, golds and reds and greens and blues—how could one not look, not read?

Unlike most American comic books, those from India had no cliff-hangers; each was a complete and contained narrative. Moreover, they did not follow the course of a single hero or heroine through a series of consecutive issues, drawing instead in one comic upon a piece of mythology, in the next, on a piece of unrelated history, telling both in ways that did not seem so different.

The books were instructive. I discovered that warriors were powerful and skillful, but that facility and prowess were overvalued. In the final analysis, battles revolved around the inclinations of the gods, who granted boons of weapons and invincibility to those soldiers who had demonstrated the greatest devotion, standing on one leg in the forest, praying, even as ants bit and maidens tempted. I learned that even the most powerful warriors quaked before the priests, like Vishwamata was forced to do before Vashisita, when with a single syllable, the sage destroyed the king's army and killed his sons. And priests, on occasion, had to be instructed by the gods—Narada thought himself the most devout devotee of Krishna till he had to walk round a hill balancing a pot of water on his head, and realized, at walk's end, that he had not thought of his lord a single time.

There were certain personalities (the Pandava brothers, Hanuman, Birbal) who would reappear issues apart, and in this way, they became older, closer friends, their latest adventures at once new and familiar. There were elements of some stories that did not make sense to an eight-year-old. What did it mean that Rama was embarrassed when a subject in his kingdom said that he was not like the king, that he would not take back his wife after she had slept at another man's home? What was the harm in a sleepover? And why was it so outrageous that five brothers had to share Draupadi as a wife? I had to share with my brother all the time.

The characters in the story lived in, moved through, spaces that I came to understand as the landscape of the subcontinent. There were elephants to be ridden into battle, tigers to be hunted for sport. People lived in palaces, because they were royalty, or else in the jungle, because they had been banished or driven from their kingdoms. Villages were small but pristine. Goats and snakes were plentiful, wives were demure and pious and faithful, miracles were commonplace, mendicants were more often than not disguised heroes.

They looked Indian in their dress, these comic book inhabitants, saris and dhotis and gold ornaments, but their skin was always bleached, as though, in ancient India, cities were populated only by peach-colored people. There were divinities who were purple and blue, but only *rakshas*, demons who battled endlessly, fruitlessly, against the *devas*, denizens of heaven, were the dark, *desi* color I saw at home or encountered on weekends, when I'd trail behind my parents at the parties they attended and collect my food (Indian for the adults, pasta for their children) on a Styrofoam plate, trying not to spill it on myself or on the carpet of whoever's house it was that I was visiting. If I were wiser at ten, I might have seized on this inconsistency and realized that India was distinct from my comic-inspired imaginings. I might have more accurately anticipated the place.

At eleven, I was skinny and eager to arrive in India. I'd been there twice before, but I remembered nothing of those earlier visits. On the flight from New York to Bombay, I steeled myself to be brave—like Magellan, who had sailed round the world, or Hudson, who had sailed up the Hudson—for the adventures I anticipated.

Bombay did not disappoint. We arrived in the afternoon and began immediately to sweat. We rode into the city in the car my mother's brother had hired. Everyone was Indian. They all had black hair and brown skin. They were on motorcycles and bicycles. They were pressed into buses so tightly that the buses bulged and when we stopped at a traffic light, a young man, sweating and mustached, riding such a bus—just barely, with his foot planted on its lowest step and a single arm gripping the rail, the remainder of his body extending from the vehicle like a side mirror—set his free leg onto the edge of our car. His sandaled foot pressed against the window. On the other side of the glass I had pressed my nose, transfixed. My mother pulled me away and banged on the window. The light changed, the foot retracted. The bus groaned and disembogued a billow of sooty exhaust. Inside the car, I took a deep breath of the fumes, horrified and fascinated at once by the smell and the feel, primal and grimy, and when we had passed on, having escaped the gas, I felt heroic. Later, I blew my nose, and found the mucus dirty and dark.

There was antiqueness to things in India that appealed to me. Monuments were too plentiful to be preserved properly and this dereliction conferred on my brother and me access to things historic in a way that would have been unthinkable at home. We touched carvings in temples, we rubbed paintings to test their color. At old forts, my father would pay the guard or the guide, quietly, off to the side, a bribe, and he would show us in turn rooms that were closed, tunnels which were off-limits, secret passages that led to crumbling bartizans, the sandstone glowing carroty in the setting sun.

Places in India had existed so long that they had outlived their histories, growing instead to occupy newer, more extraordinary stories. Battles occurred in this spot not centuries ago, but many millennia past, when three hundred thousand had died in great struggle. Beneath this peepul tree, at the spot of this shrine, a rishi had sat for one hundred and twelve years in meditation. Soon after the murti was installed in that temple, a great flood swept through the valley. Only the homes of people who had taken prasad that morning from the temple were spared. In this manner, places secured their own bit of sacredness. More honest anamneses at other sites by blue, Government of India plaques were, in comparison, humdrum.

With older cousins, I went on long motorcycle rides, my brother wedged between the driver and me. We'd dash in and out of outrageous whorls of traffic, we'd honk our horn at every opportunity. We'd ride on the opposite side of the road, because India had once been British, and we'd ride on the right side of the road, because one side was as good as another. If we parked we might return to find a cow had settled next to our bike.

If possible, we'd leave without disturbing it, but were we stuck, we'd have to yell at the cow and slap its sides till it moved, begrudging us the foot its shift bestowed. When we rode late at night or outside town, the roads cleared and we'd speed; the wind and the dust would tangle and mat our hair; my brother and I would whoop.

This India, the India that I experienced as adventure, I had been expecting, primed as I was by the books I had read. The greater part of India, though, was a shock.

The crowd—the same crowd that had made Bombay wondrous and the traffic fantastic, that spilled from out trains that seemed worn from overuse, that filled the streets, bartered in the markets, waited on long lines outside the movie theaters, the same crowd that would soon settle into my parents' home—unnerved me.

I was accustomed to suburban quiet. India was a tangle of noise—street vendors, bicycle bells, car horns, transistor radios broadcasting cricket matches. From the kitchen came clatter and the hiss of steam, the angry sizzle of oil. Babies cried in bedrooms and bassinets scattered through the house. The arguments of children, the scoldings of parents were general, as were the discussions of the men with the men, the women with the women. Only the afternoons—after lunch, when the air was warmest—were respites from the unbroken sounds of those closely clustered lives as we all slept, briefly becalmed.

My nights, too, were restless. School schedules forced us to vacation between June and August, when the vagaries of celestial orientation baked the subcontinent with a flushed and ardent heat that was relentless. We slept that summer, my mother, my father, my brother, and I, on two beds pushed up against each other and wedged into a corner of our room, above and around us a gauze of mosquito netting. We'd tuck the netting into the mattress, sealing our sleeping compartment, and while our mesh presidio kept us from angry insects, it slowed the flow of air, so that we'd sweat desperately through the night, the humidity and the heat of our four sleeping bodies accumulating inside our breezeless fortress; we'd thrash ourselves to sleep and dream quinine dreams.

I felt unsure in India of going to the bathroom, accustomed, as I was, to sitting on a toilet bowl when I had to shit. Most homes we visited had keyhole-shaped toilets, flush with the ground, footpads on either side, and squatting above the holes, I felt unbalanced. I'd often have to shoot a hand out to my side to keep from keeling over. My anatomy, too, seemed designed to sabotage any attempt to defecate, my piss always precariously close to shooting forward, wetting the underwear and pants I'd pulled down around my ankles. Most upsetting was that I was sick with chronic diarrhea for most of the trip, and four or five times a day, for weeks on end, I felt inept.

❦

I had, that summer, a recurring nightmare. On arriving in India, my parents had warned me about the poor, telling me to watch my pockets, to be careful with my watch, and not to give anything to anybody. I learned to grow uncomfortable around begging children, small and frail, who in their aggressiveness struck me as feral and predatory. Outside a temple at Mount Abu a boy, my size though likely malnourished and several years older, pulled on my shirt and motioned toward his mouth. He looked like me, but we did not notice this until a cousin of mine said, "Hey, you are either twins or you were switched at birth." Hearing this, the boy smiled, his teeth straight and white. I wrenched his arm free of me and raised my hand, thinking maybe to strike him. He stepped away, recognizing the motion, I think, moving toward another car that had arrived outside the temple.

In my dreams that summer I imagined both our lives swapped. I dreamt of my hair unwashed, uncombed, of my body caked with loam, naked above the waist. I imagined pulling on the shirts of people, desperate for them to notice me, and I saw that they had been so inured to my presence that they would swat at me, like an insect, just to be rid of the irritation I caused them. Then I saw the boy, walking with my parents and my brother, into a restaurant, an improbably situated burger joint with an attached, enclosed outdoor playground, and I tried to call the doppelgänger out. He turned and raised his hand, and fearing the blow, I retreated.

❀

"You should go back now and see what you think."

"I should."

"You need to keep in touch."

"Do you think I'd like it?" I asked Vasant and he studied my face, puzzled.

"What's not to like? It is your home. You are Indian, after all."

iii.

Some distance into New Jersey, we had pulled off the road. I bought Vasant some fries and a soda and afterward filled the car with eighty-seven octane at Mobil. Everything in New Jersey is full-service and the man who pumped gas into my car wore a maroon turban.

"What is your father's line?" asked Vasant.

"Guess," I said.

"He's an engineer, like me."

"He is an engineer," I said to Vasant. "Good guess."

"I could tell by looking at you."

"How's that?"

"I know these things about you. Something is telling me."

"What's it telling you now?"

"Nothing now. The feeling comes and goes." Then Vasant asked, "Do many Indians work at petrol pumps?"

"Some do."

"Indians were at this last pump. Did you see?"

"Yes."

"And this is common?"

"It's common enough."

Vasant seemed disappointed. After a moment he said, "Are most Indians in such work?"

"I don't know about most, but some for sure."

"My uncle had told me that we were a professional class in this country."

"Indians, you mean."

He nodded.

Before my relatives had come to this country, I remember the adult world being populated by almost one hundred south-Asian men, doctors and engineers, and their wives, some of whom were also doctors and engineers, most of whom were primarily housewives. The community, those hundred couples and their children, would associate at selected houses in small, fluid groups through the year. Biannually, though, we'd rent out a gym or auditorium at the local junior high, and for a night, the lot of us would gather and pass the time in one another's company.

During the evening preceding, in houses throughout the county, men would refine their jokes and put on their silkiest, shiniest shirts. Women wrapped themselves into saris, new if at all possible, and chose jewelry—chains and bangles and earrings and nose rings—until they were weighted down or resplendent or both.

Parents would dress their children fastidiously. Boys were fitted into ironed pants and shirts, the latter tucked into the former, the former secured by a tightly cinched belt. The girls would wear small saris or *salwar kameezes*, the saris in need of constant parental attention and maintenance through the night, the *salwar* suits, though by no means ungainly, a concession of form to function. Everyone's hair was combed or braided neatly and in the car ride over, fidgeting was not allowed.

The gatherings were the nexus of all the information that mattered, global as well as local. There would be talk about immigration laws, talk of the new government in a particular state, talk about China or Pakistan, talk about whose child had won what prize at the science fair and which colleges the graduating seniors would attend. There would be speculation among the engineers as to how much a particular doctor was making and talk among the doctors about how the engineers could only talk about computers.

There were stares at the one couple who had divorced. They'd arrive separately, they'd mingle with the same old friends at different points through the night, and no one knew how to deal with either of them. It was generally understood that he had hit her, but beyond this there was little consensus in the community. People were skeptical—every marriage has its problems; she should have stayed. People were sympathetic—thank God she had the sense to leave. Both camps followed her and her son Sunil with their eyes surreptitiously the whole night, rubbernecking at the spectacle.

❖

One year, as happened at every one of these functions, the boys (those who weren't yet old enough to want to spend their time with the girls) left an hour into the *garba* or *dandia* or *natak* (I don't remember which) and, procuring a Nerf football, demarcated a field of play between the rows of washed cars in the dimly lit parking lot.

Music seeped out of the gym into the night, rhythmic, with more treble than bass, the voices of female singers high but not shrill, the male singers' deep and warm. It was either late fall or early spring. Sides were chosen. Play had commenced, two-hand touch; two completions were a first down, five-Mississippi rush. The teams were lopsided. New sides were chosen. Everyone had to have a turn at quarterback. Sunil was the really fast kid and he was beating his man up and down the blacktop. Everyone started to sweat. Nobody's shirt was tucked into his pants anymore. Somebody slipped and fell, scratching his arm, tearing his shirt. His mom was going to kill him.

One team was kicking off to the other (though we didn't really kick, we just threw the ball as far as we could). Sunil, about to catch the ball, let it drop instead. The football bounced high into the air. There was a scramble beneath it. The kicking team got the ball back. Someone went to yell at Sunil, but he was hiding behind a car.

"I think my father's walking in this direction," he said. A silhouette had emerged from the auditorium and was now at the far end of the parking lot. "Nobody's seen me," he said and we started to play again. Sunil's father made it into the crowd of boys. We kept playing. The play ended. We huddled to start the next one. "Has anyone seen Sunil?" he asked. Loudly, "Where's Sunil?"

"I think he's dancing, Uncle," someone said. We called all the men *Uncle* and all the women *Auntie.*

"He's not inside," said his father.

"He's not out here, Uncle," someone else said. "Maybe he's in the bathroom."

Sunil's father rubbed his beard and looked angry in his silk shirt. He looked from person to person. I felt nervous and wanted to giggle. Sunil's father stared at me and I bit the insides of my cheek.

"Rajiv, you tell me, where is Sunil?"

"I think he's with his mother, inside."

Sunil's father began to nod. "Very smart, Raju, you are very smart, yes?" He took a step toward me. He smelled sharp and pungent and I thought it was his cologne. Breathing into my face, he said, "I'll find him inside, hmm?"

"With his mother."

"Very smart," he said. *"Sala chuttya."* He turned and slouched. He staggered back to the auditorium, one leg obstructing the other. When he was far enough away and I was feeling brave, I said quietly, so that he would not hear, "If we see him, Uncle, we'll be sure to tell him you were looking for him." Then Sunil was back in the

game, the ball was snapped, and he was by his de-
fender, deep.

It was at these semiannual gatherings that I began to
sense the world was growing more populated. Between
my eleventh and thirteenth years it became impossible
to attach names to all the new faces. We'd achieved
some critical mass in the years preceding and Indians
had gravitated to the area. As before, there were engineers and physicians, but there was a new diversity
also. A part of this newer immigration, the part to
which my father's family, soon to arrive, would belong,
seemed to me very different from the Indians I had
known.

They were distinct at our gatherings. I understood
this, at the time, only through the vague sense that the
new arrivals were somehow more Indian than the Indians I had known. As awkward as my parents were with
English, the language seemed even more remote for the
new arrivals. Around town, at the mall or in the super-
market, to my insecure twelve-year-old eyes they felt
like eyesores: the wives always in saris, the husbands
attentive to some obscure, garish sense of fashion, their
dialect loud and booming in an otherwise quiet public
space. I recall feeling they made me more obvious.

My father's family was, in many ways, characteristic
of this part of the newer immigration. These immigrants
were older, setting out for America not as single men of
twenty-five, but as women and men, grown, often with

children of their own. Brothers and sisters already living in the States sponsored them in their visa applications. They were less likely to be heading for universities or residencies. Though many had been educated in India, the work they found in America initially hovered around the minimum wage. They aimed to work those jobs till they amassed capital and know-how. If they were successful, they went on to own newsstands and convenience stores, gas stations and motels.

A peculiar relationship developed between the world of older immigrants I had known and these new, nonprofessional arrivals from India. Individually, the newcomers were someone's sibling or cousin or aunt or uncle, and were afforded the respect and attention that the relation demanded. There was also, however, among the older immigrants the sense that something was being lost as the community grew. With significant numbers came a balkanization, and being Indian began to matter less than where specifically in India a person was from. This, though, was a familiar impulse and perhaps not so distasteful to many as was the notion that the lens through which the nation viewed the populace as a whole was changing. It was discomforting to a group so proud of its successes that it had become an ethnicity of taxi drivers and shopkeepers. That older, wealthier community began to define itself more narrowly. So when Vasant's uncle told him that Indians in the States were a professional class, he wouldn't have felt he had misrepresented the situation. He had a particular sense of who were and who were not his peers.

When I was twelve, in the days before my uncle and aunt arrived from India, my home was reordered. New photographs, of my grandparents, of my father's family in India, were framed and hung; a charcoal pencil nude was hidden in my parents' closet. Statues and paintings of our gods were moved from obscure to prominent locations throughout the house. Bologna and hot dogs were removed from the refrigerator and consigned to the trash; my brother and I took cheese and chutney sandwiches to school.

I missed beef but we were Gujarati and we were Hindu, so it would not do for my uncle and aunt to see us consume the flesh of cows, in our home no less. On occasion my father would secret my brother and I from the house to visit McDonald's, the three of us enjoying cheeseburgers and Big Macs, but even these times we'd have to brush in the restaurant bathroom after eating, applying the toothpaste from the travel-sized tube my father brought with him to our teeth with our fingers, for fear the stench of sin would linger on our palates, foiling us all when we returned home.

I did not note, at first, the increasingly tepid nature of our nighttime viewing. It seemed only as though we were settling on newer shows whose plots and characters might be more appealing to my relatives. It was later, some weeks into the change, that a reason for the switch became apparent. We had been watching a television program together, all of us, and as it neared its end, the actor and actress edged across the screen toward each other. The camera zoomed into their faces, their lips close and moist. But before the kiss, my father changed the station, searching, he said, for some news. It occurred to me then that in the same way it made me uneasy to watch a love scene, two lovers writhing suggestively beneath satin sheets in a candlelit room, with my mother and father, they, in turn, were uncomfortable watching a man press his lips to a woman in the presence of my uncle and aunt. I was told this explicitly a week or two later: there were shows I was not to watch if my relatives were near.

With the arrival of his sister and her husband, my own father seemed smaller in his house. Part of this effect was physical—my uncle was taller than my father and my aunt was wider—but it had more to do with the way in which my father seemed suddenly subordinate in his own home, his pronouncements about things pedestrian— what we would eat for dinner, where we would spend the weekend—no longer definitive. When he would grow angry and yell, my brother and I were still afraid of his authority, but in other ways, he appeared cowed by the presence of his relations, emasculated, almost.

✻

On my thirteenth birthday, I had a party. My friends and I played video games like Zaxxon, we ate pizza and cake and I got presents. When finally it was time to go home, my friends sat lacing their sneakers as, my parents chatted with theirs. Tim's mother was by to collect him though he lived only three streets away—he was an only child, and she was a single mother, and that was the way things were between them. He was leaving the living room when his foot hit against a book that lay on the floor, and he pushed it away with a kick. Climbing the stairs, up toward his mother and my parents, Tim was caught by the collar of his New York Giants T-shirt, my uncle holding him tight.

"In this house, Timothy," said my uncle, "it is the worst rudeness to touch a book with your feet."

Tim's mother, watching, said nervously, "Sorry, he didn't realize. Say 'sorry,' Timmy."

"Sorry."

"Don't tell me, tell the book," said my uncle. He did *pranam* to the volume, pressing it to his head and holding it then to the sky.

Tim's mother was staring at my uncle. He passed the book to her son. Tim looked at me. His mother had turned to my mother and my mother said nothing. I looked pleadingly at my father and my father looked away.

Tim's mother said, "Just do it, Timmy," so he did. My uncle relaxed his grip and, free, Tim bounded up the stairs and with his mother left without saying good-bye.

❋

Though there was nothing offensive in my cousins' conduct, at times their simple presence was unsettling. They were, in those first few months after arriving in America, unemployed, and without a car or access to public transportation, it was all they could do to wander about our home. When their parents, who had returned briefly to India so that certain business matters could be settled, came again to our home, I ceded the common spaces in my house to the five of them, and resigned myself to the room I shared with my brother.

I had hoped, on news of their impending arrival, that I would be close with my cousins. It was clear, however, from the second day of their arrival, when they replaced the tape a girl in school had made for me, a girl who for the next three weeks would be of high import in my life, with another, the new sounds jangly and foreign, that we did not share a common cultural currency, this though I was Indian, though they were living in America. Within days we stopped watching network programming altogether, our nights instead passed with rented Hindi movies, movies I found at the time relentlessly inane and painfully lengthy. Too, I did not understand Hindi, so I was forced to follow the films through subtitles or live time translation, my mother or father recounting every two minutes what was said, what was happening.

Language separated me from my family as well. I had lost most of my Gujarati by the time I was ten—the cumulative effect of television and school and neighborhood friends. I could understand the language but could not speak it and so exchanges with my cousins were frustrating and truncated; my Gujarati was as awful as their English. With our leaden tongues it was too arduous a task to interrogate one another. We learned to disregard our approximated lives and even in that confined space, our interior worlds were mostly separate.

I made good grades, because that is what Indian boys are supposed to do. I did not date, because that, too, was what Indian boys were supposed to do. I took tabla lessons and joined an Indian youth group. We went on family trips, nine people in a minivan, and I was miserable. I did well in science fairs. I understood that I was to be a doctor, or an engineer, or else I should get an MBA.

On weekends, my family would watch as I played soccer, left halfback though I was right-footed, the quickest kid on the field. Like the other parents of children on the team, when it was their week to do so, my family, my mother and father, or else a cousin or an uncle or an aunt, would bring oranges, cut into quarters, for our side to eat at halftime and they'd help out with the car pools to and from practice. During games, they'd shout encouragement, and my opponents and their parents would mimic their calls back to me, twisting their immigrant cadences and linguistic emphases into shrill farce. I'd grow angry at the taunts and then angry with my family for not speaking more clearly. I'd become embarrassed by them and then, more ashamed for my embarrassment, I'd slow to a jog and, winded, ask for a substitution.

I imagined myself with a name, anglicized, that was easier to pronounce. I wondered if the girls I went to school with thought of Indian guys as guys or as Indians. And later—when I'd let someone else's tongue into my mouth, firmer, more muscular than I had expected, and felt, that same night, my first breast, small and yielding, sequestered in lace—I ruminated on arranged marriage.

I recall feeling as though situated in a demilitarized zone between two nations, my own allegiances unclear. Times when these two countries would meet, I felt perpetually nervous that one side would commit some breach of etiquette, egregious, unforgivable, that would forever doom them in the eyes of the other. Accordingly, I lived in a way that separated, as cleanly as was possible, the groups from one another, spiriting my family from my friends, my friends from my family.

I thought of India often. Days I felt removed from my family I'd remind myself that it was clear that in India my brother and I were visitors, tourists, *firang*, lucky if we emerged from the bathroom clean, our crap and urine deposited without occasion.

But there were days, too, numerous, often strung together so that they became weeks, where I'd dwell on a slight against myself or my family—immigration difficulties, job difficulties, language difficulties, and snide asides—and wonder if we weren't better placed in India, where the sun bleached everything except skins, where my grandfather had bombed his bridges, where we'd all be less obtrusive.

My father's relationship with his family was inconstant. There were occasions when it seemed they made him whole, that he could not be without their presence, these brothers and sisters, these nieces and nephews, and now, too, their children, who would refer to him as *Dada*, "grandfather." When the family was assembled for an occasion, Thanksgiving, Christmas, my father felt a deep satisfaction in their sheer numbers. He had effected their translocation, he had reduplicated his world in his new country, and perhaps now this place might begin to feel like home.

But this clan was also a group deserving of near-constant worry and remonstration. Their failures—to get good jobs or good apartments, to decide against higher education in favor of what it seemed were an endless series of ill-considered business schemes— became his own. He would berate my cousins about their tortuous progress, their lack of material success. His constant critique coupled with his relative prosperity made my father into an unwelcome curmudgeon. Months would often pass, as a dispute raged through the back channels of uninvolved kin, when my father would fall out of favor with some person in the family.

In this way my father was a frustrated man, his America most familiar when populated by Indians, the Indians he loved less than accomplished, less than fervent, in pursing his American dream.

Dear Father and Mother, dear Chotuji, dear brothers and sisters, dear nieces and nephews,

Jai Shri Krishna!

What wonderful news. I can only imagine, sitting here in my room, what my newborn nephew looks like. Does he look more like bhai or bhabi or is that a question I should not be asking?! He will be five or six weeks old, I expect, by the time you receive this letter and you will have decided on a name, but let me make my suggestions just the same and treat them like guesses. My preferences, if you begin with M, are Mukesh, Mohan, and Mahesh, in that order. Also Manu. If you begin with Dh, I like Dhiren and, to be quite honest, am not so keen on most of the rest. Now, if you have picked an alternate Dh name, do not be concerned, I am sure I will learn to love it well enough.

You must all be wondering already about the car advertisement. Quickly then, the photo is a fair representation of Vijay's new car. In fact, Vijay's car looks better than the image I have enclosed. His parents sent him the money for the car after Vijay wrote home asking for newly tailored clothes. He sent them his measurements and they called him at the college. They asked if he was well, if he was eating. He said that there was not so much to eat. His parents asked if they should send food from India. Vijay explained that the customs officers would not let foodstuffs into the country. Then his parents asked Vijay, is there nowhere that you can get good food in America? Vijay replied that there are some places in New York City where he might purchase the right ingredients, but there is nowhere local. The next day Vijay's parents phoned again to tell him that they were sending money for an automobile so that he might go to and from New York City regularly. Can you imagine their wealth? In any event, I am well served by Vijay's distress. If he loses some more weight, I might be able to procure tickets home.

We are making good use of the car. We went to visit Suresh two weekends past and this last Friday we drove to Ithaca in New York to visit Vinod. He seems to have settled himself well and after spending the evening at his place we left the next morning for Boston. Vinod knows a student there doing his doctorate in physics and we stayed at his place on Saturday night. We saw some of the city the next day — mostly those places near to the university and it seemed to me the place for a thinking man. You wonder as each person passes, particularly the ones that look as though they might be faculty at the colleges and universities, what occurs inside their heads. Vijay says this is stupid, that they have the same thoughts that we have — what to eat, that it is too warm or cold, what errands they must complete before returning home — but this, to me, seems all the more extraordinary.

We did not complete a tour of the city because we had to return Vinod to his place before returning to Newark. He has already seen a number of places in the country and his opinion was that compared to Washington, D.C., there was little to see or do in Boston.

"Washington just feels powerful," he said. "The streets are wide and the buildings are enormous. If feels like New Delhi but somehow less misplaced. The monuments alone convince me that this is a country committed to greatness." Now, I have not yet been to the capital, but with that description how can I not visit? Vijay and I will go there this weekend.

Vinod said to us as we left him at his home, "If you have brains, you will go to Boston. If you have ambition, you should go to Washington. But if you have both, only New York will do."

Vijay said to him, "I don't think Ithaca counts as New York."

I asked him, "What if you have neither?"

"That is what Newark is for," he replied and we all laughed. Then he said, "If you have neither intelligence nor drive, this is not the country to be in."

"Washington has made quite an impression on you," I said.

"No, it is true," he insisted. "Otherwise, we would be better off someplace else."

"We will be someplace else, no?" I asked him.

He shook his head and said, "I am going to stay in America."

Vijay and I discussed this issue after we had left him for the better part of the next three days. We cannot understand his decision. If you meet his parents, please do not inform them. Vijay and I will convince him to return, I am sure of it. I'll write more soon.

Love,

Vasant

Four

i.

Because my third day in India was cool, the Kwality shop was empty and Ba and I had our choice of seats. She ordered herself a chocolate milk shake and I had a frozen mango bar. Nobody bothered us as we sat and ate. The ice cream parlor felt something like a beach town in the winter, in a hibernation of sorts. Just out from the door, though, the street was still active. The store owner, a tall, mustached man in his forties, sat looking out the parlor's front window, and that clear but not clean glass admitted the sights and muffled the sounds of the world outside. The owner's life seemed strangely bipolar, fractured by a shift in season, hyperactive, then somnolent.

"Do you want a bite of this?"
"I don't like mango. Take some of this?"
"Okay."

A child, eight or nine, was using a tired rag to wash the store's tiled floor. Squatting on his haunches, he'd dunk the rag into a blue plastic bucket of water and use the saturated cloth to rub and polish. Satisfied, he'd shuffle himself a foot backward and start to clean the next piece of ground. The owner watched him disinterestedly, once shouting at the boy for some offense. The boy nodded without looking up from the floor and continued with his work. His threadbare blue clothes looked like a hand-me-down, unadorned Cub Scout uniform.

Ba asked, "Do you miss your father, Raju? I think you must. Do you know, even when he would come to visit, even then I missed him. How to enjoy someone's company when you are counting the days until they leave?" Ba sucked on her straw.

"When your vacations had ended, your mother and father would sit in their room, packing all the things they had bought, always struggling to make everything fit, weighing and weighing their bags, to make certain they weren't too heavy for the plane.

"I hoped they would miscalculate. When they arrived at the airport, they would be told their bags were too heavy. The next flight would be full. All the flights would be booked for weeks and you all would come back to me. This was my hope, even after I found that if your baggage weighs too much, they just charge you a little bit extra money. I have missed your father for thirty-two years now. I miss them all." Ba was quiet and I thought that for her to watch the family she had grown leave her must have been like watching a life's work dissolve itself.

❧

Ba finished her milk shake before I had finished my mango bar and she ordered a second. "It is not healthful, I know doctor*ji*. Tell me, how is your medical school?"

"It is interesting," I said.

"Good interesting or bad interesting?"

"Good interesting."

"Your mother wanted to be a doctor."

"I know," I said and then I asked, "Did you ever want to be anything, Ba?"

"I wanted to be a good wife."

Two customers had entered the store. The woman wore a shirt that said San Francisco on it. The man's shirt had a polo horse over his heart. They ordered a banana split. It was served and they ambled, leaning against each other, past the boy scrubbing the floor into a booth near ours. They fed each other alternating spoonfuls. My grandmother stared at the couple.

When the milkshake arrived Ba slurped it down and rose quickly, paying the owner of the store as she hurried out. "Let us go home before your grandfather returns. I have a surprise for you." So we clambered along the street, my Ba racing around obstacles, past carts and cows and people and pigs. Her sandals slapped against the pavement in a staccato rhythm.

In her room Ba unlocked her cupboard and removed a small tea tin she had nestled behind her sari blouses

131

and beside a framed photograph of my extended family taken during Thanksgiving, six years ago. She took the tin to her desk and pried off its lid. The pile of letters, folded and packed tight, sprung from the box like convicts from a prison. My grandmother said, "Your father used to write his first few years in America, before he had the money to phone. I have saved some number of his letters. I could give them to you."

"Yes?"

"But they are written in Gujarati. You cannot read Gujarati, no?"

"No."

"But I could read to you."

"Yes?"

Ba nodded.

"Early on, it took half the night to read your father's letters. The mail would arrive in the afternoon and whomsoever was home would take turns holding the letter to see for themselves that it had come. We would guess what the letter might say, but not until your grandfather came home would we open it. When he had returned from work and had something to eat, those who were home would assemble in the drawing room. Your grandfather sat on a chair and all others sat on the floor. In those days there were twenty-two people living in the house. To arrange and quiet all of us was like a great military operation. Finally, your grandfather would open the envelope and read us what your father had written. Before a sentence was finished, everyone would call aloud and try to anticipate what your father might have to say. Often we were wrong but frequently we were correct.

"Everything he wrote we tried to imagine. In those days, information on America was not so easily available. Everyone would tell what they knew, from rumor or radio or *National Geographic*. Slowly we began to see the place around your father. We would argue about everything he had written. If your father described a building, everyone would have a picture of some building in their mind and we would all talk to each other until someone mentioned a structure in town that we all agreed must be like the one your father was describing. When he purchased a camera, this became easier. If he described a food, we argued until we agreed we had estimated the taste well enough. Sentence by sentence, this is how we read the letter.

"When we finished, the discussion was half completed. During dinner and then after dinner we would together compose a letter to him, mentioning all the changes around us so that he would know what was happening in his absence. Your grandfather decided what was important and then wrote your father a reply. We would all add a line at its end."

Ba began to read me my father's letters. She held them in both hands, pieces of unlined paper, blue aerograms, too, black ink. We sat on the floor and her elbows rested on her thighs. Her white sari was draped over her head. She wore small square glasses on her round face. Ba's voice was warm and strong and filled the room with its colors. When the text demanded, Ba simulated emotion and action to match the words in the gestures and faces that my father had learned from her, and the letters felt corporal and recent. When later Ba heard the sound of my grandfather's steps on the staircase, she gathered the letters together and replaced them in their tin. By the time my grandfather entered the apartment, Ba's treasure was hidden and secure in her cupboard.

ii.

The sky opened impulsively my fourth day in India and rain, precipitate and severe, milled the city. The power failed then returned then failed again and when the sky cleared Ba and Bapuji and I went out to wander.

Water had tamped the town and those things not stone or cement or asphalt were soggy. But the ground had been dry before and it spirited the rain away to stores hidden, dark and deep and underground. I imagined the water's movement, that reverse percolation, as its second fall, parallel to the first, but delayed and infiltrating another world.

It felt, after a long, confined morning and afternoon, like a reprieve to be outside. We had drunk cup after cup of tea, played card game after card game, shuffled between the two rooms, and still it felt as though not a thing had occurred for seven hours. The rain past, though, the city began to reassert itself. Shuttered windows were opened, umbrellas collapsed and people appeared from beneath them, pedestrians replenished streets. We passed a greeting card store that seemed busy.

"Is there a holiday coming?" I asked Ba.

"Listen to the music," she said. "Christmas is coming." She pointed to a Santa Claus in the shop window. "You see that? Your father would send us Christmas cards twice every year. During December would come a card that said 'Merry Christmas' and during Diwali, the cards that said 'Seasons Greetings' or 'Happy Holidays'. I think each Christmas he must have bought an extra batch of cards and saved them to mail in October. I discovered this only these last few years, in the time since our local stores have begun to carry these Christmas cards."

"There are twenty Christian families in this whole town," said Bapuji grumpily.

"So?"

"So how did it come that everyone is celebrating Christmas?"

"Tell me."

"It is the same reason all these children are wearing blue jeans and T-shirts."

"There is always room for another holiday."

"Now we all need to buy Christmas presents."

But Ba would not meet his mood and asked, smiling, "What will you bring me?"

In the direction we walked, around the southern edge of the city, the buildings yielded briefly to an inlet of countryside and then continued undiminished on the far shore of green. There was centered in this piece of displaced farmland a small and shallow pond and as the road we were on condensed into a footpath, we found ourselves walking beside it.

I remembered the pond from the summer of my last visit to India. It had held three water buffalo, their black hides covered with mud, their horns thick, curled along their ends like professorial mustaches. Gripping the ropy tail of each buffalo was a child with a switch. They counted to three in unison. They swung their sticks briskly and there was the sound of a wet smack. The hides of the buffalo quivered locally. The animals snorted and their nostrils flared. They pushed away from their positions of repose, the water parted before them. It streamed beside their muscled hulks. A tail-length behind followed the children, skimming over the water surface, their heads and noses visible, their bodies submarine. They were laughing and shouting and when the buffalo came to rest in the shallows, the children clambered on top the animals and began to scrub them with fresh mud. The buffalo grunted approvingly and the water in the pond stopped its sloshing.

In the market, vendors would wave flies away from their carts as buyers investigated their comestibles. When the transaction was complete, a price agreed upon, the food weighed on an iron balance scale and packaged into newspaper, or alternatively when the buyer passed on to another cart in search of fresher, firmer food, the shooing would stop, new flies would resettle. So Ba and Bapuji and I caused minor diasporas as we moved between stalls, procuring our night's dinner.

Ba was expert in her haggling. She approached the carts and picked idly through the foodstuffs. She'd ask for a price. She'd find the least-favored piece of produce on the cart, a sorry, stunted growth that must have been neglected by both the rain and the sun, a specimen bruised and ugly and overripe, and look up, evidence in hand. A lower price was offered. Ba would frown and turn away. She would be asked to come back. She would resist. She would be asked again. She would return, impatient. A third price would be tendered and Ba would accept. I would collect the food for her, carrying it away in the thick cloth bag she had brought from home.

I was struck that morning, as I would occasionally be struck the entire time I was in India, by the notion that the town was brown-skinned and black-haired, that their facial features approached my own. There was a solidarity, unexpected, unreasoning, that I felt with the people I passed on the street. They were, during these moments, my people, and though I had my difficulties with the subtleties of their language, though our manners of dress and thought were distinct, though, perhaps, these people that I passed did not regard themselves as bound together in any particular way, at these instants I would disregard such nuance and imagine a profound relationship between us. Later, during stretches more lucid, I'd marvel at this rush of emotion and wonder as to its source.

A procession of cars, muddy by their wheels, Ambassadors all of them, passed alongside us on the street. They honked and we yielded. Ba looked into one of the vehicles and smiled and a man inside smiled back. Bapuji caught sight of the man and when the man waved, my grandfather did not wave back.

"Was that Chotuji in the car?" I asked.

Bapuji shrugged. "I did not see," he said.

I helped Ba make dinner and though I was, in the kitchen, more an obstacle than anything else—constantly in the wrong spot, laggard in my peeling of the vegetables, my eyes needing respite from onion cutting, the *rotis* rolled too slowly, too fat, or otherwise too thin, rarely in a shapely circle—she was happy to have the company. She made me sing an American song for her, not believing me when I said mine was not a singing voice, and then, when I had finished, said, "I think our Indian songs are better, no?" Through the rest of our preparation Ba sang songs and melodies distantly familiar, as though I had heard them last in the womb, tunes, it seemed, that were lodged in some primitive part of my mind, the same part that controlled breathing and heart rate, the part, if insulted, that would leave my fingers cold from lack of blood, would leave me apneic and screaming for air.

❧

After we had finished dinner Bapuji stood up and said that he was going out.

"Where?" said Ba

"I have some business to see to."

"What business?"

"My own."

"I have no money for you, not a single rupee."

"Did I ask for anything?" said my grandfather, but it was false bravado, because he did need money. He asked me to come with him while he commandeered a rickshaw and once we had left the house said, "I must be losing my mind, I've forgotten my wallet in the flat. Raju, would you go and get it for me?" As I turned to fetch it he thought better of it and said, "No, you won't be able to find it. Better that you give me two hundred fifty now and I will return you the money when I have come home." But I only had hundred-rupee notes in my wallet, so Bapuji had to take three hundred.

Ba and I watched a show on television and then began and finished a game of chess. Ba read a newspaper in Gujarati and I read a paper in English. When it came time to go to bed, I unrolled my bedding and moved it beside Ba's bed. She gave me a sheet and a pillow.

"Raju?"

"Yes, Ba?"

"I cannot sleep the whole night through, Raju." The

lights in the room were out and Bapuji had not yet returned. "I am falling asleep at my regular time but I am waking earlier and earlier."

"Do you feel sick?"

"No."

"You feel well otherwise."

Ba said, "I don't feel that way either."

iii.

The morning edging into ripeness found Ba seated on her bed, reading an article in the paper. Bapuji called in to her, "You will be late."

"What is the time?"

"Almost nine."

"Then I will be late," she mumbled.

"Don't keep God waiting."

"What does God have if not time?" said Ba, but she had already folded her paper and unfurled her legs, slipping her feet into her sandals. She checked and adjusted her sari and, satisfied, unlatched the door and sighed down the stairs, off to the temple, reluctantly pious.

The telephone rang while I was bathing, and the noise of the bell, high and clear, metal on metal, sounding in doublet peals, felt brazen in the comparative quiet of our two rooms. My bath finished, I returned to Ba's room to dress and observed my grandfather seated by the desk upon which the phone sat, heavy and plump, black with a rotary dial, his hand pressing the receiver into his face. His conversation was hushed and, observing my interest, Bapuji sent me into the kitchen to prepare some tea.

❊

Bapuji and I left the apartment before Ba had returned, before the tea was finished, immediately after he was off the phone. Once again, we were into the streets, walking briskly, and we took our first rest before a jewelry store. I looked in through the store window at the displayed bridal adornments, the necklaces and earrings, weighty but finely wrought. In the case was the laminated photograph of a woman, a model dressed as she might on her wedding day, thin and fair, with aquiline features and large, soft eyes. She had deflected her gaze toward the ground, demurely, but her half-upturned face was an invitation, unmistakable, for aspiring brides and for desirous grooms. Noticing how my gaze lingered on the advertisement, Bapuji told me about his own marriage.

"Your grandmother, she was not yet fourteen and I was twenty-two but she was smarter than I." Bapuji brushed a fly from off his eyeglasses. "Now, in these modern times, the boy and girl, they will meet and talk before marriage, but in that time, I knew only your grandmother's town and her father's profession. My parents had decided on her and though I had been taught to trust them, I was not the trusting type. I told my brother, your Chotuji, to take a horse cart to her town and by some means, he should try and see Ba.

"Three days after he left, he returned home, very sad and serious. He took me aside. Our father must be in

143

debt to Ba's father, he said, because there was no other reason for me to be betrothed to such a homely girl. And the food she cooked! Chotuji said it was as though she had mixed cumin with dust and wood bark—he could hardly swallow the concoction. And, he added, there must be a forest nearby to judge from the size of her, a forest whose trees had been stripped of their bark.

"I was distraught. What to do? I spoke very little to my parents before the marriage. They thought me nervous rather than angry. Still, I held my tongue out of respect. When I saw your Ba, then, on the day of our wedding, I thought I had been blessed. She was dressed in a sari of vermillion red, she had *mehndi* on her hands and gold in her nose and in her ears. She looked perfect. I wish I had a single photo from that day. As it is, I must refresh that memory from time to time by dwelling on it. And if the girl from my mind was to stand tomorrow beside your Ba on our wedding day, I am not certain who would be prettier.

"I told you that your Ba was clever, yes? The first thing your Ba said to me, she whispered during our wedding ceremony. She asked, Do you take your wood bark with butter or without?"

My grandfather had concluded, but for a moment after he finished speaking, he stayed, in places private, with the story. His spine straightened and his chest swelled and lost in his past, his face was the least burdened I had seen it since arriving in India. Then he returned, reconciled himself to the present, and we were off walking again.

Some streets over, men in tight, flared slacks or else in loose kurta pajamas, their hair slicked back or else vanished, overweight or slight, these men had clustered democratically around certain stores, their postures easy, arms around each other's necks and waists. I noticed this as we walked away from the jewelry shop and I mentioned it to Bapuji.

"Cricket match today," he said. "We are playing New Zealand."

"Who is better?"

"We are better. Who will win, who knows?"

We walked a half mile further and Bapuji stopped finally outside Bharat Switches and Electronics. He led me into a group gathered around a small black-and-white television in the storefront. The men, almost all twenty or thirty years younger than my grandfather, surly-looking, I thought, welcomed us into their circle. We watched quietly for some minutes and then Bapuji asked, in English, "Do you follow?"

"Not really."

The shopkeeper, Bharat, asked, overhearing "He's not from here? London? America?" Bharat was approaching sixty, his face beginning to slide off his skull and into his jowls.

"New York," answered my grandfather.

"Does he speak Gujarati?"

"He can try."

"Do you follow cricket in America?" he asked me.

"No," I said, wanting to say more but wanting also not to make a mistake with the language.

"You follow baseball and basketball there, yes? I have seen these games on the television."

"Yes, baseball and basketball and football."

"Are you liking India? Does it suit you?"

"I like it."

"My sister is in Georgia. She is married to a doctor there. She has been there in the States now for twenty-two years. She is a pharmacist. I have been to visit her two times. They took me to see Washington, D.C., and Atlantic City and New York."

"I live in New York."

The man nodded. He turned back to the game and said to my grandfather, "It is the same way with her children. It is like trying to talk to a wall." Bapuji nodded and my face flushed.

We stayed at the television and Bapuji explained the game to me. After a few minutes, the television commentary switched from Hindi to English and the slowness of the uniformed men on the field became more interesting. Still later, an Indian player, Tendulkar, took a great swing and knocked the ball through the air. We followed its projectile path till the ball landed behind the farthest line, six points. The crowd in the stadium erupted and we, in the street and the store, began to jump up and down. Bharat, whose sister was in Georgia, clamped his hand round my waist and we kicked our heels into the air, not nearly in unison, but trying.

Afterward, Bharat decided Bapuji's explication was inadequate and he scattered the men from around the set into the street. They took up positions. Bapuji made me the batsmen, found three sticks to serve as wickets, and became the baller himself. He pitched imaginary spins, I applied imaginary strokes. The mustached men in the street fielded the imaginary strikes, their sudden starts and pivots creating knee-high clouds of dust. When traffic appeared, we moved to the side of the street and waited impatiently, like children, for the inconvenience to pass. One of the wicket sticks fell to the ground and I was declared out.

When we returned to the match on television, Bapuji and Bharat disappeared into the back of the store, leaving me out front with the other men, men who seemed kinder now. They peppered me with questions about American sports and American actors and actresses. Still unsure of myself, but feeling more confident, I answered.

Later Bapuji and I waited, under a billboard advertising a film, for the bus. The painting showed the hero and heroine and their nemesis in the Himalayas. The title of the film dwarfed the mountains. The actor had on sunglasses, the villain had a scar and stubble, and the actress wore a tight shirt and a smile.

We boarded the bus for home and I paid for our two-rupee tickets. The bus was old and seemed a hazard. I noticed a sign painted onto the splintering wooden back of the bench seat in front of us. English letters ran beneath Devanagari script in faded red: "Please look under your seat. There may be a bomb. Notify the driver. Earn a reward." Bapuji told me not to worry because the city had bought these buses used, from Delhi.

Dear Father and Mother, dear Chotuji, dear brothers and sisters, dear nieces and nephews,

Jai Shri Krishna!

How to describe the week just passed? Vinod's mother's brother's wife's nephew is living in Chicago. Though the city is fourteen hours distant by car, Vijay and I decided to accompany him on his trip. The Monday just past is a holiday in America so Vijay and I rushed our students through the laboratory on Friday afternoon, met Vinod who had taken a bus to New York, and left for Chicago at five that evening.

We drove in shifts, so that one person slept while the other two were awake. It was my turn to drive at three in the morning. You know that I can stay awake late into the morning without difficulty, so I told Vijay to have some rest. Vinod was already sleeping. When I was the only one left awake, because this country is vast, and there are parts of it that are a great wilderness, I began to feel as if I were an explorer, like Marco Polo or Ibn Batutta. What must they have felt crossing a desert or a jungle, not knowing what sights awaited them? I concede that the life of a student of engineering is not the same as that of Livingstone or Stanley, but all the same, it has its rewards. True also that it is unlikely that any great navigator ever had a heated automobile and the sounds of a radio to keep him company, but just the same, this is how I was feeling. It was in this mood that I decided to drive to California.

Both Vijay and Vinod woke several times through the night and into the morning to ask if I needed to be relieved but I sent them back to their slumbers. It was well past ten o'clock when both woke fully, oriented themselves, and understood where we were. I had driven with some speed and Chicago was three hours gone.

They shouted at me for some time. I told them that I wished to see California.

"Absolutely not," said Vinod. "There are people waiting for me in Chicago. If I do not come, they will think we have crashed."

"Absolutely not," said Vijay. "We have laboratory to prepare for on Tuesday."

"We will call the college and tell them that in Chicago our car has broken down. It will take one day to be repaired, then we will be back. What will they do? Only delay the laboratory for a day. We will work double shifts on Wednesday. What of it?"

"But my cousin . . ." began Vinod.

"You tell your cousin that our car has broken down in Newark and that you will make it some other weekend."

"Why, so that we may drive to California only to turn around and return home?"

"For that reason exactly," I said.

"It is a good reason," said Vijay.

"You see," I told Vinod, "there is now a majority for California."

"Now we are voting? There is no vote. I need to go to Chicago."

"We are in America—democracy and all that. How do you vote, Vijay?"

"California."

"I myself vote for California. That leaves only you, Vinod."

"Let me find a phone to call my cousin," he said and so it was unanimous. We drove in shifts, without break except to buy fruit, bread, and cheese. We passed through the states of Missouri, Oklahoma, and Texas by Saturday, and on Sunday we crossed New Mexico and Arizona. In the middle of the day on Sunday, Vijay was driving and Vinod was sitting beside him. Vinod woke me from my slumber in the back seat and pointed to the distance and told me to look. There is, in certain parts of America, a great and empty flatness to the earth, the ground as level as a lake for miles to the horizon, and because of this we saw a storm approach. Understand, we did not feel it growing windy or notice that it had become overcast, we saw the clouds as they marched across the sky like angry soldiers in formation, a perfect, roiling line, and when the storm reached us, it attacked like an army. Rain fell in frozen pellets even though the temperature was warm. The wind screamed at us. Thirty minutes later we had made our way through and, emerging on the other side, the sky blue overhead, we pulled to the side of the road and looked back to watch the commotion before continuing on.

Besides this, however, the weather was gentle. During the day, we drove with the windows down. The rush of the air through the car blew anything not sufficiently heavy through the cabin. At night, we rolled the windows up to lock in the heat and we listened to the radio when we could receive stations, sometimes to music, sometimes to discussions, sometimes also to religious sermons. This country is more pious than I had imagined.

By early evening on Sunday we were nearing the California border, but, after all this travel, decided to save the state for another trip. Instead we drove to a small city near the Hoover Dam and there passed the night without event.

The next morning we woke and after a brief stay in the city traveled to see the dam. It is a marvel of engineering. The turbines are as tall and wide as temples and the concrete itself rises from the base of the river it stopped to the lake it created like a smooth mathematical function.

We drove home without rest, starting that Monday afternoon and not reaching home until Wednesday at noon. Vijay and I showered and left Vinod in our apartment. When we had finished teaching our laboratory classes we returned home, thinking to return Vinod to Ithaca, but the three of us fell asleep, exhausted. Today is Thursday, and Vijay has gone alone to return Vinod, leaving me with some time to write and study. I will send another letter soon but just now I need to get back to work. I hope all is well and I wait for your letters.

With love and regards,

Vasant

ive

i.

Interstate 80 loped through the low Appalachian hills like an unfurled bolt of cloth. Vasant and I sped along its asphalt, my passenger not realizing that my route, from the Van Wyck, across the Whitestone, haltingly through the Bronx, traversing the George Washington, south on the Turnpike heading toward Newark, then, as the city approached, northwest on 280 toward Parsippany, was not the most direct.

"What about your girlfriend?" said Vasant.

"How do you know I have a girlfriend?" I asked, turning to look at him. Vasant shrugged his shoulders. "This is America."

"I'm single. I broke up with my last girlfriend in October."

"What was her name?"

"Anne."

"She was American?" he asked.

"She was white," I replied, understanding the question.

"How many girlfriends have you had?"

"Since when?"

"Ever."

"I don't know. Six or seven, I think."

He said, looking concerned, "But you will marry an Indian girl finally?"

"It could happen," I said.

"It is your preference?"

"I'm not sure I have a preference."

He said, "It must be your parents' preference."

"That it is."

"That is why you are no longer together?"

"I don't know."

When I graduated from college, I lived in a house with four other guys, one of them Indian, the others white. Our graduation ceremonies extended through a May weekend, starting Saturday evening, ending Monday morning, and we planned to have our families come up the Friday before, to have dinner and to meet each other. The guys living in my house were friendly with the girls living a few houses down and we decided to all go out together. My girlfriend, Anne, with whom I had spent the last two years, to whom I would precipitously, four months later, propose marriage, lived with those girls down the street.

One of us made reservations for thirty-eight people at an Italian restaurant we'd never eaten at but was the sort of upscale place—decent food, unreasonable prices—that families treat themselves to at graduations. Two days before, Sanjay's parents called to say they wouldn't be able to make it up until Saturday, so we called and changed the reservation to thirty-six.

My parents and my brother arrived first, at four in the afternoon. They sat downstairs in a living room that had been fastidiously cleaned the evening before. Everyone from the house came by to say hello. My father was tired from the drive and after talking for a bit went upstairs to my room to take a nap. My brother, my mother, and I went to walk around campus.

My mom needed every building explained. What was it? When was it built? What went on inside? Could we look? She would name the trees and the flowers and the bushes. She'd see all the things that I hadn't noticed in four years at the place, how all the statues were named. She loved the libraries best. "What can all the books be about?" she asked.

My mother was impressed by the institution, a repository of learning and scholarship, the kind of place she had missed the opportunity to attend. To her this was holy ground, a place that could lead to all the lives she had abandoned when she had chosen this one. Too, there was a satisfaction she felt in having her child attend a college such as this one, the same school to which people more wealthy and famous and powerful would send their own anointed offspring.

That house my last year of college was typical of off-campus student housing. It was old, but not so old as to be distinguished by a historical plaque. It was three stories high. The five of us paid thirteen hundred in rent, or rather our parents shared the sum. And though ours was not the worst housing available, the interior of our house—its furnishings scavenged from the Salvation Army, cleaned once or twice a semester—could not but feel some degree of dissolute. Still, it was the first house that any of us felt could be called our own and when our parents arrived, we were proud to show them around. They were proud that we were all graduating. We served them wine and beer, gin and tonics, and scotch and sodas. Everyone was dressed smartly. By six, all of our parents had arrived and Anne called from her house to tell us that everyone there was about to head over.

It was a peculiarity of my relationship with my parents that we never talked about the girls I had seen. They understood that I had dated, but they were unconcerned with the details and, for my part, I saw no reason to burden them with the information. From this my parents discerned that my relationships were not so serious and I was able to convince myself that a girl non-Indian, or non-Gujarati, or nonselected might be agreeable to them. When Anne's parents met my own, I felt no awkwardness. Perhaps she did.

The evening began easily enough. The parents mingled with their children and their children's friends. Conversation centered around plans for after graduation and traffic on the ride up or down, depending on whose parents were talking to whose child. Anne's parents briefly met mine. They talked about the house we lived in and speculated on what it had looked like two nights ago. My folks asked about Anne's plans after graduation (she had none) and Anne's folks asked if I was ready for medical school. Then, after a few minutes, people, our parents included, disengaged from the conversations that they were in and rearranged themselves in the room with new talking partners and the same talking points.

At some point during the conversing and switching, my mother developed, as she did upon occasion, a migraine. When everyone's family piled into cars to head to dinner, we dropped my mother off at her hotel room. We all offered to stay with her, individually and collectively, but she declined. My brother, my dad, and I hurried to catch up with the others for dinner. When we arrived, most of the seats had been filled already. Rearranging everyone seemed an inconvenience. My brother and I sat together at one end of the long table the restaurant had arranged for our party and my father sat at the other.

My father had a few drinks before we'd left for dinner, but he could have a few drinks. They relaxed him. He'd grow convivial, worrying less about his word selection, assuming people could understand him. My dad was not a large man, however. Neither was he a drinker, except for social occasions, and this left him open to miscalculation.

My father sat next to Anne's parents and Anne, and

next to them were Josh's folks. Just around the time the appetizers were served Josh's parents and Anne's parents hit it off. They had both read the same biography of Teddy Roosevelt. They talked about Rough Riders and trust busting and imperialism. When my father mentioned a photo he had seen of Roosevelt and Churchill and Stalin when visiting Hyde Park, everyone paused awkwardly for a moment before they switched their conversation to accommodate his mistake. My father recognized, by the break and the sudden shift of subject matter, that of the two Roosevelts, he had chosen to remark on the wrong one. Embarrassed and quickly lost again as the conversation turned to a play on Broadway that it seemed everyone but he had seen, my father refreshed his drink and excused himself from that end of the table to say hello to my brother and me.

Sanjay was sitting next to my brother, and next to him was Dave. Dave and Sanjay were both Yankees fans, and they speculated with my father about the Yankees chances that year (decent) and whether Mattingly could make the Hall (maybe, but probably not). Eventually he returned to his seat.

Anne, sensitive to my father's discomfort, sought to include him as he sat down. She mentioned a book she had read on the Mughal era in India and asked if he had seen much of the architecture, knowing already that he had. My father mentioned the Taj and raved about Fatepur Sikhri, the emperor Akbar's now deserted capital city. He told her a story about Birbal, Akbar's wisest advisor, and how he had once resolved a land dispute. Then, perhaps, noticing that none of the people around him seemed drawn or connected to his stories, he grew quiet again, asking Anne absentmindedly and for the second time that night what she planned to do after graduation. After that, conversation restarted in an alternate direction. Frustrated and disinterested, my father drank, smiling and nodding the whole while, until he was clumsy and soused.

By the time coffee was served, the restaurant had emptied except for us. My dad stood up and waited till everyone was quiet. "Sorry to stop everyone's talk but I wanted to say a few things," he said. "First, that I am very proud of all the children here, who are graduating from college and have made everyone proud and have also organized a very nice dinner." At this, there was general applause from the parents. "Secondly, a toast to my son, who has made me very happy in particular. Finally, a toast to his mother, who is as responsible as is anyone for this happy, happy day, and to his brother, who would tolerate him as he was growing up." Everyone clapped again and when my father sat down, one by one, the other parents at the table stood with toasts of their own. Someone made a collective toast for all of us that were graduating, thanking our families, and it was after this that my father, much to everyone's bewilderment, stood again and asked for someone to sing. "The Beatles, anything, any song you like."

❦

It was an intimate gesture. In my family, at the end of nights when everyone was together for a weekend after a long while apart, we'd sing. The songs would be festive or melancholy, religious or *filmi* music, little snippets of something stuck in their memories. People were off tune; it didn't matter. Others would forget words; someone would remember for them. They would sing till they were exhausted, everyone discovering everyone else's voice anew and recalling the circumstances of the last time or the first time they heard the song. My parents and their friends would arrange music parties. Someone would sing, someone would play the tabla, and someone would carry a melody on the harmonium. They'd listen and drink and when a maudlin verse was particularly powerful, they'd shout out, *"Va, Va,"* in appreciation. The alcohol had helped my father into a warm place, melting away the degrees of separation he felt from the Americans around him, till he felt they might all sing together.

No one sang. Everyone was confused. They waited for more. Was it a joke? Was he serious? "Maybe when we get home, Dad," said my brother, hoping to give my father a way out.

"No, no, here!" said my father. "We have the whole restaurant to ourselves!"

No one moved and I repeated what my brother had said. "We'll do it at home, Dad. Okay?"

"Come on, come on! Who wants to sing?" said my father. Everyone looked down at the table, at their cups of coffee and their desserts. My father looked around, understanding. He was alone and he retreated. "At home is fine. I didn't mean to force anybody."

Sitting, he hit his chair off center. Trying to stay balanced, he grabbed for the table and managed both to avoid a fall and to knock over a cup of coffee. Anne's mother yelped as the liquid reached her. A stain spread over her restrained and tasteful ankle-length linen skirt.

"I'm so sorry," said my father. "So sorry."

"Not at all," said Anne's mother, not looking up. "Accidents happen."

My father winced, because with this concept, he was familiar.

The year he died, my father had to buy a new car, and so he went to dealerships, gathered brochures, read *Consumer Reports*. He spent well over a month collecting information and, in the end, processed the data through an algorithm he had developed, hoping for a particular outcome and receiving another. He repeated his calculations and, deriving the same answer, set about collecting new statistics from different magazines. He tweaked his formula. By week's end, the scientific method had yielded another result, one more satisfactory to my father, and he went on to buy the car he wanted. My mother, who watched the whole process with frustration, kept me informed by telephone. My father, in separate conversations, represented his thinking as a model worthy of emulation, rational and relentlessly logical.

The purchase was clearly improvident. My father's job was insecure, my brother and I were in school. At my mother's insistence, however, we bought the car my father liked. She understood the purchase as necessary. Her husband had wrecked his last car in a miserable accident.

My father was alone during his crash and though afterward he felt the fault was not his own, he was unsure of this. He'd try to reconstruct the event and though each of the reconstructions reassured him, they did so with varying degrees of probability, so there were hours and days when my father thought his accident might have been, partly, slightly, his fault, and, by corollary, avoidable.

What occurred, we think, is this. In the second week of March, the weather warming but slowly, my father had been working harder and longer hours. His job, he felt, depended on a demonstration of his indispensability. As the day began to grow long again, my father found himself returning home later and later, so that each evening, he would drive on the cusp of night. He employed his headlights, but probably relied more on the day's last, lingering light. He was not an incautious driver, however, neither would he have been vigilant — he had made this drive five days a week, infrequent sick days and more infrequent vacations excluded, for twenty years. The route had always been benign.

He was almost home. My father had turned onto our street and was following it downhill. Two homes before ours, just as the hill flattens and the road curves off to the right, a girl on a bike rode from her driveway out into the road. My dad, perhaps because he was near home and tired, maybe because it was by now dark and the driveway was hidden from his view, missed that activity until it was upon him.

Mike and Shannon had lived together in that house for seventeen years. They had three children: Meghan, two years younger than my brother; Caitlan, three years younger than her sister; and Carolyn, almost seven. The girls all had red hair. My parents called them the Fire Sisters. Mike and Shannon had been over to our house two or three times during the first years that they moved into the neighborhood and I think we went to theirs about as often. For the past ten years, though, they encountered my parents only in their yard or ours, on Tuesday nights, while they were taking the garbage to the curb, or on Saturday afternoons doing yard work. Their meetings were friendly but always circumscribed, never extending into a night of conversation or a shared dinner. My parents found this the inevitable pattern of their friendships with Americans (they used this term even after they and most of their Indian friends had taken new oaths of citizenship), intercourse that was, after the first few clumsy interactions, unsustainable.

❀

My father turned his wheel hard to the left, pushing as forcefully as he could manage on his brake pedal. His tires made a high, ugly sound, like an animal's whelp. There was an incidental thud and then a louder noise as my father's car drove off the street to meet a mailbox in a violent, stentorian engagement. By the time my father emerged from his car, the neighborhood had assembled around the accident. Carolyn lay on the ground, blood seeping from her head, her leg twisted bizarrely.

"Oh, Jesus, oh, Jesus," said Mike, cradling his daughter's head, stanching the flow of red with his white shirt.

"Is she all right?" said my father.

"Does she look all right?" screamed Shannon. Her voice was shrill and thready. Her body quivered. Her hair was composed in a neat braid.

"I was just driving and she came from nowhere. She just came from nowhere out on the street. I am so sorry."

"Oh, Jesus," said Mike. "You're going to be fine, sweetie. Daddy's here. Daddy loves you."

"Mommy's here. Mommy loves you, sweetie."

"From nowhere."

Sixteen minutes later an ambulance would arrive. My father waited outside, the villain, not knowing where to stand, till it came. Someone asked if he was all right. He nodded. He leaned against a tree, his knees a little bent, his hands pressed back against the trunk. He remembered that things are regular, that in March, some trees return earlier than others, their leaves back, they ease the landscape from gray to green, they soften the sounds of the wind. He stood this way, the branches and their buds draping him, when, the neighborhood congress as an audience, Mike got into the ambulance with Carolyn and called back to him, even and composed as he could manage, "I'll make sure they deport you, you sick foreign fuck."

The police took my father's statement. They asked around for witnesses but there were none. The next day, in the light, they measured the skid marks and decided that my father's car was going about the speed limit, twenty miles per hour, when he started to brake and turn, maybe slightly faster, probably a little bit more slowly. Carolyn got better. They kept her in the hospital for four days. She had a comminuted fracture, a concussion, blood loss. My parents sent a card and flowers to the hospital room. A neighbor told them that Mike and Shannon didn't want them stopping by.

My father worked and brooded. He researched buying a new car.

One morning, readying for work, he said to my mother, "I was watching a television program last night where a man had just cheated on his wife. When he came home, he was doing all the things he does normally, taking off his coat, untying his shoes, setting down his briefcase. He saw his wife, she said hello to him. He said hello to her. She asked about his work and he asked about hers. Then, after some talk, she went to finish dinner. As he was walking up the stairs, the camera gave a close-up of his face, and he looked relieved that he had not been discovered."

"And?" said my mother.

"I have decided that this is how I feel. After living here half my life I worry if I am about to be found out. When I last through the day not feeling I have come close to giving myself away, I am relieved, like that man walking upstairs to shower in his own home."

My brother drove my dad back to the hotel after dinner and spent the evening at my house. The next day, Sanjay's parents arrived. For the rest of the weekend, my parents and his parents were inseparable, sitting next to each other during commencement and baccalaureate, at lunch and at dinner.

I asked Vasant about his plans.

"First of all, to get my master's. Then we shall see what opportunities arise."

"Do you think you might stay here?"

"I don't think I will."

"Why not?"

"My father needs help with his business."

"What sort of work does he do?"

"We have a plant that manufactures piping."

"So why study electronics?"

"I enjoy it." Vasant frowned. "It may be that I won't use my degree."

"Do you like the piping business?"

He shook his head. "Most of our contracts are government. We have to submit bids, but in truth each bid is preceded by a bribe. Too much and you have wasted money, too little and you will not get the contract. Win or lose, both ways you feel as though you have done something dirty." Vasant grimaced and said, "When I think of those things, I think I might stay here. In America, nothing can slow you if you work hard."

Columbus Day weekend, six weeks before his heart attack, I sat talking with my father and Cricket at the kitchen table. Cricket, my oldest friend, lives in his van when he can. When he can't, he works odd jobs and sleeps in cheap apartments. The jobs find him. He settles with them briefly, until he has enough money to move back into his van. The van is a '67 Volkswagen. He wears it like a badge. He uses it to follow bands around the country every time he's saved enough money to quit working. Scattered through his van are bootleg tapes of the hundred places they've played the same songs. He languishes at home, with his parents, when he has to. He's become good at this; in the five years since we've graduated from high school, he's taken care of himself in this way. Every time I see him, he is between jobs, content.

My father had just come home from work and his suit hung from his body like it was on a bent and broken hanger. For a year he'd lived with the rumor of layoffs, certain that he would lose his job, and every inch of him was frayed. His hair was accelerating to gray all over his head, gray-black eyebrows, his stubble gray-black, and gray-black strands scattered around a growing bald spot, but still combed neatly, right to left. During his last year, after long, tired days, my father would remember India fondly, wondering aloud if he should return.

On this particular day, Cricket asked my father, "So how's work, Mr. K?"

"Work is work," said my father, his shoulders shrugging.

"That's what my dad says," said Cricket.

"He must work with the same idiots I work with, then," said my father.

He and Cricket laughed.

"The thing is," said Cricket, "you guys should both just quit."

My father drank from a beer he'd just opened and said, quickly, his eyes dancing, "The problem is, we don't have vans to live in."

"You could stay in mine."

"But where would you stay?"

"I guess I'd have to get a job and a house."

"I think you shouldn't tell your father this," said my father. "He'll make me move into your van for that reason only."

Cricket and my dad talked for a while and then we left. He pushed a tape into his radio that sounded like all his other tapes. He found a bowl under his seat and we smoked as the van cluttered out of town, a tan toaster with a beaten, dented metal skin.

"Where are we going, anyways?" I asked.

"Into the sticks. It's a ways away, but they've got dollar drafts."

"What town?"

"I don't know. I know how to get there, though. Dover, maybe?"

"Where's Dover?"

"Where we're headed?"

❄

We pulled into the parking lot, the gravel loud under the van's wheels. Locking the car, I could hear music from inside. The place and the lot were surrounded by a stand of trees, thick and pretty and quiet.

Cricket and I sat down and ordered two beers, sipping and talking for a while. Cricket was talking about his summer. He followed the band he follows for two months, till they played Boulder. By that time Cricket was out of money and in need of a job. He found work delivering pizzas the same day he started looking. It was the gourmet kind, the kind the city's moneyed young lived off, and he made a killing in tips. He found a motel that rented out rooms by the week. He dated the owner's daughter for a while. Pizza that came back to the store as undeliverable went home with him after he closed up; he ate free. "I can't eat that shit anymore, though." They paid for his gas. He worked for three weeks, saving one-forty each week, and caught four more shows on his way home.

"Cricket, damn if you don't lead the most charmed life," I told him.

"You think so?" he said. "I don't know. It's not that charmed. We're twenty-three and I'm still living at home. I only want to be in this town for holidays, to check in with my folks, to tell them how my real life is going.

"Did you know I got arrested? Three weeks ago, on possession. I was parked, smoking a joint on Edgehill, minding my own, when I saw lights flashing behind me. At first it was just like getting a ticket. Gill walked up to my car and started talking to me, asking me why I was parked off to the side of the road, real friendly-like. Then he hauled my ass to jail. I tried reasoning with him. You can't reason with him.

"It's just a misdemeanor, so that's not the problem. The problem is I called my folks up to bail me out. They came down and paid but didn't stick around to talk to me. I had to call Kelly just to get home. I had to ring the doorbell to get in." Cricket took a long sip from his beer and finished most of what was left. He set the glass down on the table. "I've got to piss," he said, standing up.

When he left, I started to watch the band, tapping my fingers on the table. Cricket took his time in the bathroom. The waitress stopped by with a fresh pint. I'd smiled at her earlier that night and said something clever because she was pretty. When she set down the mug, she smiled at me. I figured Cricket had ordered the beer, but when I looked around for him he hadn't come out of the bathroom. The waitress was turning to go when I called to her, explaining that I hadn't ordered another. "On the house, cutie," she said and under my brown skin, I was blushing.

I glanced around the bar. In from the door, the bar was on the right, sturdy, five feet from the wall. The stools and the spaces in between them were full of men and women. Opposite the bar, the tables, old and wood and square, were crowded also. The floor was covered with dead leaves brought in from outside on the soles of everyone's shoes. Around the room, neon signs hung in windows, advertising beer, lighting the place in greens and blues, reds and whites, warming it with a pleasant buzz.

The stage was set in front of the tables and the bar, opposite the door. It was about a foot high, about eight feet wide. With four people and equipment on it, the space looked small and the band looked cramped.

"Did you get another? You should have ordered two."

"I didn't order this. The waitress thought I was cute."

"No shit?" Cricket scanned the bar and found her. "She's pretty."

"I wonder what the etiquette is on something like that. I didn't tip her, it didn't seem appropriate."

"You shouldn't tip her, that would make it like she was prostituting herself."

"How's that?"

"I don't know, but you shouldn't tip her. What did you say?"

"I didn't say anything."

"You should ask for her number. You're single now, right?"

"It wouldn't go anywhere."

"Because she's a waitress?"

"Because of a million things."

❋

The same day Anne and I quit each other I had asked her to marry me. We were out for a picnic, out in a big circle of a field. Around its circumference were about forty picnic tables, each next to a barbecue grill, about twenty-five feet between them. In the center was a big grassy patch where families would have been playing Whiffle ball and Frisbee if it were summer. It was early September, though, and it was a little cool to be outside, so the park was near empty. The clouds were high and sparse, the sky was a thin, scratchy blue. Anne had her brown hair all loose, so that when she turned too quickly in any direction, it would fall over her face. She'd brush it away like it was a distraction.

This park was almost empty. I was carrying a brown paper grocery bag, full of food. We'd gone shopping before we'd come out, stopping in at an A&P superstore. We bought premade hamburger patties, some mustard and ketchup, a bunch of buns. We got potato salad and potato chips. Anne noticed a special on Busch twelve packs, and seeing me wince as she picked it up, she said, "You won't taste it after the third one, anyway." Halfway to the park, she said, "So we have charcoal, right?" We didn't, so we turned around, went back to Home Depot, and got some charcoal, a little lighter fluid.

We were drinking the beers, and I was pouring the charcoal onto the grill, when Anne asked me, "You've got matches, don't you?"

"Sure I do. They give them with the bag of charcoal."

"You're joking, right? They don't give them with the charcoal."

"Oh."

She kissed me on the forehead. "That's all right, finish getting the barbecue ready and I'll go borrow some matches."

"From where?"

"Over there."

Anne stopped at a grill about a hundred feet away and was talking to a woman. Two kids ran around the both of them. After a minute or two, Anne was laughing with the woman and in another minute, she was waving to me, calling me to come over.

When I got there, Anne said, "Raj, this is Lynn; Lynn, this is Raj." Smiling at me she said, "Lynn wanted to meet the genius who thought the matches were included in the bag."

"How are you?" I said.

"Matches would make sense. God forbid anybody made anything convenient," said Lynn. She was our age. Her hair had been bleached blond. She was skinny and she wore pale, worn jeans and a red shirt. She had a friendly, throaty voice.

"I thought so," I said. "But I guess that might be a fire hazard, huh?"

"Fuck no!" said Lynn. "I spent about half an hour trying to get these things lit." She ashed her cigarette into the grill. "It's like they make them fireproof."

Lynn's two kids came from nowhere, squirting each

other with pistols. "Hey," said Anne. "It's too cold for water guns." But her opinion was of little import. They positioned themselves around her, as though she were a shield, and she was hit from both sides by streams of water. "No fair!" she said.

"Welcome to my world," Lynn said happily.

We were back at our table, eating the burgers, when Anne said, "I think her older kid is six. If she's our age she was seventeen when she had him."

"Maybe she's older."

"I don't think so. Crazy."

"There are crazier things. Don't you watch television?" Then I said, "People become as old as they need to be. My grandmother was fourteen when she got married. She spent her sixteenth and seventeenth birthdays in jail. A year after she came out, she had my uncle, the one in California."

"What was she in prison for?" asked Anne.

I had stretched out on the ground so I was flat on my back, squinting up into the sky. Beneath me, the grass felt soft, but against my neck, touching my palms, I could feel the individual blades, sharp and distinct. Anne lay beside me, watching the sky, and felt herself drifting. So I told Anne the story. I told her about the bridge, about my grandfather and grandmother, about my grandfather's brother. When I finished, Anne said, "You love that story."

I sat up and I said, "I think I might."

❊

Anne kissed me. We stayed in the park for a long while, the both of us, watching the sky. We finished the Busch, the park emptied, and long after everyone had left, night noises replaced day noises and I asked her to marry me.

"That's the beer talking," said Anne.

"What if I was serious?" I said. "Let's pretend that I mean it."

At fifteen, while watching *Mississippi Masala,* that movie where Denzel Washington and Sarita Choudhury stumble through a black-brown relationship, my father and I were sympathetic to different characters. I developed a crush on Ms. Choudhury, the first Indian woman I had ever seen bare her breasts on the screen. The idea of young love, of sweaty love with Sarita, appealed to me. My dad sided with the aggrieved father, Roshan Seth, exiled from Uganda, stuck in some forsaken Southern town, uncomfortable with his surroundings, distressed that his daughter was dating a black man. My mother hated the movie. She had heard of a similar thing happening the year before to a friend of a friend on Long Island. Her daughter married a black boy she had met at college. She couldn't imagine the wedding. Worried both by the burgeoning romanticism they detected in their son, my parents sat me down.

"Understand, your studies are most important. There will be time later, when you are a doctor, to find a wife, to settle down. Before then, but, you have to be very careful with Americans," they cautioned. "They will get married and the next day, they will be divorced, and on the third day, they will go and find another. With Indians, marriage means something."

This was part of our immigrant canon, how my mother and father raised me to understand America, how I was to remember India. Americans, their women and their men, were unstable and their loves fickle. Though it was rarely mentioned in such bald terms, it became a failure of sorts for parents when a grown child would marry someone white. At the wedding, most of the community would smile sympathetically and then contemplate the particulars of the impending divorce as they drove home to more virtuous families.

My parents' understanding of the differences between Indians and Americans extended beyond this. Indians were committed to education, Americans were not. The Indian family was strong, the American family weak. Indian children understood the value of respect, Americans did not. To argue that Americans had found a different way of living with different rewards was futile. For my parents these were questions of virtue, natural, unchanging.

When I explained to my parents that summer after graduation about Anne, they were disappointed and worried. My father said, "*Beta*, it is better that you should end this thing. Love and marriage are not like these Americans advertise. It is only new and wrapped in plastic for a moment."

When Anne and I met, the evidence seemed as though it was overwhelmingly in our favor. We liked most of the same books and movies; her favorite albums were on Matador. We were friends before we slept together, and though we were young, we did not feel green. I was thinking about these things when I asked Anne to marry me.

When Anne refused, she was understanding, I think, that we were, neither of us, ungrounded; and though, while we moved and lived in certain spaces, the separate histories of our two worlds did not seem opposed, at other times they were irreconcilable. She did not enjoy the ways in which she had become, on her first visit to my house, quiet and deferential around my parents, nor that I was glad for her modesty. She could not understand the need I had to keep our lives secret for so long, the embarrassment I felt in being so entangled.

My parents' house has a deck just off from the dining room, upstairs, raised above the grass, and beneath its floor, in its cross beams, each spring a robin would build a nest and lay eggs, three or four. The eggs were beautiful. They were small and blue. My brother and I would watch the bird and her eggs through cracks in the deck floor and later, when the eggs had hatched, we would watch her chicks.

One spring there was a storm that blew the nest from its nook, down nine feet to the ground. After the rain a slick of bloody pulp and eggshell stained the lawn. By afternoon it was covered by ants. The next spring the bird built her nest again, like the deck wasn't haunted.

I asked the waitress, Karen, for her number before I left, and I scribbled it onto the edge of the napkin under my beer. Cricket and I finished that last round; I folded the napkin in half, checking first that the number was still legible.

When I returned home that night, my father had been awake, finishing, at that late hour, work that he had brought from the office. I drew myself a glass of water and sat beside him. "Cricket's logic is the luxury of being white. Maybe he doesn't need to work. Indians, though, we have to work. That is all that connects us to this place. Without work, I have zero claim on this house or this half acre. Without our work, our taxes, our money, we could be washed clean of this country and not one person would care. I need my job." I wanted to disagree and my father sensing this said, "Your skin will always argue with your passport."

Dear Father and Mother, dear Chotuji, dear brothers and sisters, dear nieces and nephews,

Jai Shri Krishna!

This fall semester has begun and is progressing smoothly. I have little difficulty with my laboratory sections and my own research is advancing. My health is good and the weather is fine.

Some news, now, regarding the events just passed. The two men from our building who were arrested have completed their trials and are awaiting sentencing. Both were charged with a list of crimes but Evelyn explained to me that the arson charge was the most serious. She expects that they will spend ten years in prison but I hope the charge will be less severe.

There is more reliable news, now, on the unrest. It seems a Negro gentleman was arrested by the police and then beaten badly in the police station. News of this incident spread through our community and a protest rally was organized at the station. Several people from my building attended, but with work to complete, I stayed home. Near midnight two alcohol bombs were thrown at the headquarters and soon afterwards, the looting and rioting began. The following evening the disturbance enlarged and the authorities arrested more than four hundred people. It seems some number were shot dead as well. Through the weekend, the violence came and went. Some two thousand policemen were involved in quelling the area and because they were white and the whole of our community is Negro, they felt not unlike an occupying army.

I knew the two boys by their faces only, having seen them as I entered or left the building, but Vijay had several interactions with them, each time friendly. Once, he had twisted his ankle on the way home and they carried him up the stairs to our flat. Another day, when it was too warm to sit inside, Vijay sat speaking with them on the front steps to our building. Even still, Vijay is entirely unconcerned with their fates. Some change has come over him. He has said several times, "They are all animals." He repeats this frequently, in Gujarati, even when Evelyn is near, and it makes me feel as if I were on a plane again.

"What if I had taken a different way home? Or what if I were delayed for one hour because my experiment needed the incubation time? Then I would have been stuck in the jungle with these wild animals. How do you think they would treat me?" He asks me this question, or some variation of the same, every two or three days.

I think he is very scared and while I try to reassure him that he is safe, I am not so convincing. I see that most of the violence was against property, but I spent three days frightened, not leaving my flat. Our street was unmarked; still I could hear the noises of the riot and I could see the smoke. There is a frustration here I do not understand.

If Vijay chooses to shift flats, I will have to shift with him, though to do so seems to side with the wrong group in this dispute. It is poor precedent as well. Shall we commandeer a building and allow only graduate students from India to live by us?

As the summer ended Vijay and I left the city and traveled to meet Vinod. Together we went to visit Niagara Falls. The three of us took a boat up the river to the base of the falls and the sound was so loud that talking was useless and we could only make faces at one another to express our wonder. When we stood above, watching the water plummet, it felt as though the ground was drifting and I was forced to look away from the falls and grasp something solid to assure myself that the earth and I were fixed and in fact our motion was only a trick of the moving water. I wait for your letters.

Love,

Vasant

Six

During dinner on my fifth day in India, when I had asked about my grandfather's brother, Ba and Bapuji said nothing and stared past each other, dwelling on the food they were chewing like cows considering their cud. Bapuji swallowed first and said, "He is about, doing those things that he does."

"How is he?"

"How is anybody?"

"He is well," said Ba, ignoring her husband. "He would be happy to see you."

"Raju will need to make an appointment," said Bapuji.

"If you have nothing of sense to say, it is best to remain silent," said Ba. Then, to me, "We will go tomorrow to see him, after we have finished breakfast."

"Every morning Raju and I walk together," protested my grandfather.

"Too much routine makes a person uninteresting."

The next morning, we hired an autorickshaw, a two cylinder, three-wheeled, canopied taxi. The driver sat above the engine, which he started like a lawnmower. He steered and accelerated and braked with handlebars. His horn buzzed like a giant angry bee. Ba, Ba-puji, and I arranged ourselves behind him, slightly cramped and uncomfortable. My grandparents both sat back on the padded bench seat and between them, I fit by sitting on its front edge, my face closer to the driver than to my grandparents. They said nothing to each other and though the driver tried to speak with me, my language doomed the enterprise. Thus made a peculiarly quiet foursome, we proceeded to meet Chotuji.

Overhead, the frame of the auto was covered with a thick, plastic-coated cloth. Its sides were open to the road and it was through these openings that I managed some sense of our movements. From the old town we emerged, as though through a canyon onto a plain, into the new city. The older city was narrow and vertical, the newer city was broad and flat. The roads, though wider, were no more ordered. The old city's streets were crowded with people and bicycles and animals, scooters and motorcycles. The newer city had complicated the situation further with cars. Without lanes, the traffic moved in a loose and fluid tangle, and the distance we traveled forward felt small in comparison with the distance we traversed from side to side.

The homes were sculpted concrete, each compound separated from its neighbor by cement walls, the cement anchoring iron gates which opened to give access to the street. Over some walls an occasional tree was visible, suggesting a private and interior lushness. We arrived after thirty minutes at Chotuji's.

❈

The bridge bombing had been the start of Chotuji's ascent. After his release from prison, bruised and lacerated, my grandfather's brother found himself the unexpected beneficiary of nationalist favor. Bewildered, Chotuji, too, was invigorated: he had been given purpose, inadvertently but clearly. With the zeal of a new convert, he joined Congress. He began wearing only homespun. Student leaders from the university began to stop by the house. "For tea only," Chotuji would tell his friends, his smile meant to invite disbelief. He committed himself to the cause and the party was not coy— the more he involved himself, the higher he rose in its ranks. By the time of Independence, ten years after the bombing, when Ba and Bapuji returned from their exile with two new children, Choutji was well established. My grandfather tried to join him but found the party had little use for revolutionaries. They needed diplomats, finished, careful men who understood practicalities, who were, above all things else, politic.

And so, my grandfather was eclipsed; his brother advanced from minor local posts to major local posts and finally, in seventy-four, to the state assembly. Though three times Chotuji found himself implicated in scandals and schemes, his mistakes were not so egregious to warrant his removal from office—a basal level of corruption had come to be expected from elected officials. When he retired, friends who ran newspapers published glowing appraisals of his tenure.

❧

"*Arre*, look who has come," shouted my grandfather's brother. He stood in the doorway to his home, an impressive and modern-looking structure of smooth and curving cement, his minor Guggenheim. Steps descended from where he stood to a smallish yard bordered by shorn shrubs and flowering plants, everything green still wet from a recent watering. The drive into his house was the orange-red color of packed clay and it lapped against the more serious and industrial tar on which we stood, looking inward at him and his éclat. "Open the gate, open the gate!"

Bapuji glared at the guard, who stumbled as he tried to be crisp and nimble. From one of India's northeast provinces, the man had a face that seemed to me more eastern than southern Asian. He was young, younger than me, with a gentle suggestion of hair on his upper lip. What the man lacked in size he had made up for with asperity, making us wonder for a time if he would even announce our presence inside. Stepping into the compound, my grandfather said, gesturing to the watchman, "The idiot would not let us in."

"Sorry, *bhai*, he is new and he is still learning. That is no excuse, though," Chotuji said loudly, so his guard might hear. "You give these people any authority and they use it without discretion." Then, turning to the man, Chotuji said, "You have been inside the house, haven't you?"

"Briefly, for a moment."

"What, briefly? Yes or no?"

"Yes, sir."

"How many photos of this man are in the house?"

"I didn't notice, sir."

"Start noticing."

"I will, sir."

"It will be your job, otherwise."

"Yes, sir."

Walking in toward the house, I asked Chotuji how long the man worked for him and when he said, "Six or seven months," it occurred to me that it had been at least that long since my grandfather had visited his brother.

People glided into and out of Chotuji's drawing room as though they were skaters on ice. A woman with water for everyone was followed by a man with a message for my grandfather's brother and he was followed by another woman who deposited a plate of snacks and chutneys in front of each of us. Periodically, each would reappear, with more water or more food or more notes scribbled, and then again would disappear, withdrawing from our company into some hidden recess of the home.

It was perhaps the inactivity that such care facilitated rather than sloth that had led to Chotuji's impressively rotund figure. Ten years younger than my grandfather, one year older than my grandmother, Chotuji looked a full decade younger than his seventy-one. He had dyed his hair so that what had remained was oiled and black. The pounds he had accumulated served him well, stretching the skin overlying so wrinkles were muted and undermined. Too, the weight he bore lent gravity to his posture such that when he sat, he seemed to have made a decision not to move or be moved. When he did rise and walk, the ponderous movement seemed a degree inevitable: he would be neither rushed nor turned.

"Did you know," Chotuji asked me, "that I was the one who convinced your father to go to America?"

"Really?" I said.

"Your father did not need any convincing," interrupted Bapuji.

"A push, then, in the appropriate direction," said Chotuji. "After his graduation, your father couldn't get any of the positions he had hoped for. The best jobs went to students who had scored better on their exams or who were better connected. For three years your father was working in a factory that made televisions."

"Radios," said Bapuji.

"Radios, televisions, whatever. There was no future in that work. So I said to your father, why don't you go to America and get a degree from an American university. That will open some doors for you here. Your father, he was thinking this already, but he knew your grandfather would not let him go."

"Who told him to go if not me?"

"After I convinced you, yes. Your grandfather still believed in that nationalist nonsense," he said to me.

"What is it you would say, that India is a universe, her great strength her moral character that a trip to the West could only corrupt?"

"As I recall," said Bapuji, "you believed those things as well."

"In 1937, *bhai*, maybe in 1947. Not in 1967. And certainly not today. In any case, I wrote some letters, I got your father his applications, and when he had been accepted, we set about convincing your grandfather. Eventually, everyone agreed that he should go, get his American degree, and then come back to India. I thought he might be away two years, but that country, that country seduced him. He was a simple boy from some backwater town in India and Hollywood America got him." He shook his head. "Perhaps even then I realized that he didn't stand a chance."

Later, during lunch, Chotuji asked me, "Are you a cricket enthusiast, Raju?"

"I'm becoming one. Bapuji and I watched yesterday's match on the television."

"It is an intoxicating game."

"Do you play?"

"Look at me. You tell me, how many old and fat men have you seen playing cricket?"

"I've only been watching for a little while now and I haven't seen many games."

"Sidestep, sidestep. Forget this medicine, there may be a politician in you."

"Don't wish that on him," said Bapuji.

"The reason I am asking," said Chotuji, ignoring his brother again, "is that I have been asked to attend a match in Ahmedebad. I have an extra ticket."

"I'd love to go," I said.

"Who said I was inviting you?"

I apologized.

"Don't apologize. I am joking." He laughed and looked around for an audience. Someone who had moved into the room with sweets smiled with him. "Of course I was inviting you. India's junior team is playing against the West Indies. We'll go together and afterwards, I know a few people, maybe we can meet with the players. It is something to see, a cricket match. Take some sweets. I cannot, you know. Diabetes."

"When is the match?" asked Bapuji.

"The morning after next."

"No good, Raju has made a commitment already."

"To whom? Maybe it can be rescheduled."

"No," my grandfather said firmly. "Perhaps on another occasion."

"I see," said Chotuji, staring at his brother. "Very well, Raju, I will notify you in advance in the future. I had no idea your agenda was so full. Next time, then."

"Yes, next time," agreed my grandfather.

Ba and Chotuji and I talked idly. Bapuji was silent. Afterward, Chotuji offered us the services of his driver and my grandmother accepted his munificence. We rode home as quietly as we had come in Chotuji's Ambassador, the newest of his three.

Bapuji was agitated. Returned from his brother's home to his own, he busied himself cleaning the place. He pulled a whisk broom from some nook and, squatting, swept the floors of both rooms of his apartment from corner to corner. What little dirt had accrued since Ba's cleaning, four hours before, he gathered into a newspaper and deposited outside in a trash can. That task finished, he retired to his room, which seemed to him, all at once, in disorder.

"This place needs to be cleaned," he announced. He set to removing the books from his bookshelf, alphabetizing them before he wiped the dust from their jackets and replaced them in some more particular arrangement. Though his room looked unchanged to me, he surveyed the space around him saying, "Better, better."

When he entered Ba's room and began considering the content and the comeliness of the objects on her shelves, she interrupted his brown study. "Thank you for your attention, but my room is fine just as it is."

"It is dirty."

"It is not."

"You haven't been cleaning."

"Then what do I do all day?"

"When Raju and I return, this flat should be without a blemish."

"You shall find it however you wish to find it."

In 1952, two years after CK Birla founded Hindustan Motors, India completed its first general election and Chotuji was elected to his first office, Commissioner for Water and Water Services. That same year my grandfather had another child, his fourth, and shortly after that birth, three months after the conclusion of the elections that had swept Nehru and his dream of a secular and socialist nation into office, my grandfather, still dressing in homespun but frustrated by the incessant triangulation and concession that democracy demanded, perhaps overshadowed by his younger brother as well, attended his last meeting of the Congress party.

That same year there was a strike in my grandfather's city. Forty-six textile men had been picketing their place of employment for nine days when management, irritated and feeling obstreperous, secured a group of *goondas*. These thugs, poor men paid a mercenary's fee, armed with rods and steeled by a home-brewed alcohol, were driven to meet the disgruntled laborers. A melee ensued and a loom man was killed, blows to his chest fracturing ribs, a slow seep of air collapsing his lungs.

Bapuji was hired by the union, fledgling and disorganized, by an accident of propinquity. His was the office closest to the plant and his sign was familiar to those workers who could read, who each day had passed it on their way to work.

My grandfather sued the factory's owner for damages and won a substantial reward. The day after the verdict was announced, my grandfather was pictured on the second page of the city's newspaper. He stood — skinny and bespectacled, in a barrister's robe and a powdered wig — exultant between two union leaders. They held his arms high over his head as though he were a prizefighter who had just won a bout.

After the case Bapuji loosed himself from the wealthier, less virtuous clients upon whom his practice had once relied. Too, he grew apart from old friends. He made less money and moved into a smaller office in a poorer locale. He furnished the place with a desk and a chair and some shelves for his law books.

I've wondered, since the theft, about the things a man with four young children might consider before changing his life so radically. When I am inclined to think about stealing the Ambassador kindly, I am certain that there was a moral lodestone that set my grandfather's course and he, beholden to its direction, followed its imperative relentlessly.

Other times, though, I am certain Bapuji was aware that he had begun to command esteem in a way that he had not since he was a saboteur. Fourteen years past he had a cause, he had adherents and compatriots, but having left behind organized political activity, settling back into the comparative sedateness of family life and competent but uninspired litigation, these choices might have found my grandfather wondering at the ways in which his days had grown weighty and inert. Then, suddenly, he was a headline. And it's possible that his midlife metamorphosis had as much to do with the desire for recognition, the promise of appearing in newspapers again, as it did with civic inclination. To acknowledge this is only to say that his new way of life, more austere, detached from the community he had known, was not without reward.

The benefits were, to my father, less obvious. When he was nine, on Diwali morning, a rickety gray horse driven by a rickety old man pulling a rickety wooden cart bursting with color arrived at their house. The driver announced that the wagon and its contents were for my grandfather's family. My father and his siblings swarmed around, inspecting its loot, finding all kinds of gifts and firecrackers. When my grandfather, confused, emerged from the house and learned the cart was a goodwill gesture from a factory owner against whom he had filed suit, he turned the driver and his load away. The children returned to the house, the possibilities of the kaleidoscopic dray lost to them. My father, heartbroken as only a child who has been given a gift only to have it taken away can be, turned on his father. "For the sake of three dirty, lousy leather workers, you have ruined everyone's Diwali."

Bapuji, who had been walking to the house, wheeled round. He slapped my father across the face three times, hard. "I will certainly ruin your Diwali, Vasant."

And so my father experienced the holiday locked in the bathroom, listening to the sounds of the house and the city in celebration. When his mother brought him his water, he refused. When his siblings brought him sweets or offered their company in commiseration, he refused them, too. Late at night, when his father came to let him out, spiteful, seething, but unable to lash out, my father refused once, the only protest available to him, saying that the bathroom suited him quite well, thank you.

Then, when Bapuji made as if to lock the door again, my father began to cry. My grandfather picked him up and carried him to his room. His son sat upright in bed as Bapuji fed him and stroked his head. Around him, his siblings feigned sleep. My father apologized, sniffling, gulping down his food. When he had finished eating, Bapuji pulled the sheets up around his son and sang and rubbed his back until my father fell asleep.

Leaving the apartment that afternoon for our morning walk my grandfather was indecisive about where we would go. He started left out of his door and then wheeled round. He stopped at intersections as if he were new to the city, weighing the consequences of each turn.

❈

I stopped with Bapuji outside a small temple, a *mandir*, dedicated to Ram. Two ghee lamps were lit beside the door to the place. Smoke rose from the flames in thin, dark wisps and collided with the transparent air, curling, then dissipating. From somewhere inside, a bell was beginning to sound, thick and heavy, announcing the start of prayers. People rushed past Bapuji and me, stopping for a moment to remove their shoes and sandals before hurrying inside.

"I think they will start darshan soon," said Bapuji.

"Should we go inside?"

He shook his head. "Your Ba comes daily. Has it done her any good?" Bapuji sighed and said, "I am feeling tired, Raju, let us rest here a moment," and so we stood a long while, listening to the prayers inside conclude, watching as the people emerged from the temple with fresh tilak on their foreheads. The air grew colored, a deep and royal blue as afternoon slipped into the dark of evening, and through this air, cool and light and still, the smells of the evening's dinner, cumin and tumeric, roasting wheat and deep-fried peppers, reached us. Then, when it seemed entirely quiet inside the *mandir*, and the only sounds on the street were the noises of distant rickshaws and cars, of bicycles rattling over cobblestone, then, with surprising suddenness, Bapuji slipped his feet free of their accoutrements and stepped, barefoot, into the *mandir*. "You wait here," he said, and I nodded, but when he had passed from sight, I removed my shoes and followed.

❋

The building was crude and small and the open courtyard into which Bapuji had stepped was only thirty feet square. But off to the right of the space were a set of ten long, high stone steps which opened into another room and at the far end of this room, twenty by forty, were two closed doors of carved wood plated with gold and encrusted with stones beautiful but not precious. On the other side of these doors, hidden from public view except at times of darshan, would have been a statue of Ram, and next to him, his wife Sita. The couple would be flanked by Ram's devoted younger brother, Laxman, and supplicant before the couple, with his hands folded and his tail trailing from his back, would kneel the monkey god, Hanuman, Ram's most loyal servant.

But the doors were closed, the idols hidden from view, and my grandfather stood, alone, he thought, his eyes shut, his hands clapping an even and steady beat. He was singing a devotional softly, so that his music seemed adherent to his body. As he sang, his head swung from side to side, unhurried and fluid. Then Bapuji's hands began to clap more quickly, and the motion of his head swept over the whole of his body, and his feet stomped on the ground. His voice sounded out, bold and full and deep. The flames of oil lamps spaced about the room began to flicker and dance, my grandfather beating on the air, the air beating on them.

✤

I slipped from the room as Bapuji finished his song, before his eyes opened, while he stood motionless and exhausted. I tiptoed from the room and through the courtyard. I replaced my shoes and waited for my grandfather. When he emerged, his face was glistening. He slipped on his sandals and we began to walk home.

"I should buy your Ba a gift," said Bapuji.

"I think she'd like that."

"I can do this much for my wife, at least."

"What do you think she'd like?"

"Make a suggestion."

"But you know better than me what would make her happy."

Bapuji frowned. "A new home, to live with her children in America. Nothing that I could give her."

"I know what Ba would like," I said.

"Tell me."

"Buy her a Christmas card."

Bapuji shook his head. "I cannot."

"Then how about a New Year's card?"

"Let us look," said my grandfather, but when we reached the gift card shop, it had already closed, so we returned home empty-handed.

iii.

"In America, Raju, this is the sort of room in which they perform scientific experiments. A single particle of dust would bring the ruin of months of investigation. This is a high-technology room." We had returned home from our walk. Bapuji was feeling apologetic. "I think," said Bapuji, "that I see the chief scientist of this laboratory." He approached Ba but she did not look up from the cinema magazine she was reading. "She is an extremely busy woman, the top thinker in this entire facility. Perhaps she will talk to me. The last time I was here, she had security throw me out into the streets. Take care not to disturb her." He stood in front of her and pulled down her magazine. "Madame, a few questions if I might: how does a room come to be this free of filth?"

"Some people find it very dirty," she said, shifting in her chair but not looking at him.

"Impossible! Only a simpleton could make such a mistake."

"Agreed."

Bapuji tapped her shoulder and she turned to him. "It really is a very clean house."

"I know it."

"My mood was off." He stroked her head. "I am feeling better now."

"Good, then."

"My grandson is hungry."

"Sit and see what this scientist can prepare."

Ba cooked and Bapuji and I played chess. When I had lost and dinner was ready, the three of us sat together to eat, points of a triangle arranged around the food. As each person concluded the meal, he or she would begin speaking more, and like a conversation in the round, each night a spare, quiet dinner progressed into a louder, less languid communion. This night we talked and ate until it was late and it felt time for each of us to read quietly before we fell asleep. But Ba said, "Let us do something."

"We can watch television," suggested her husband.

"Something else."

"It is nearly ten," said Bapuji.

"Even so," said his wife.

"Raju?"

"I'm not tired. Full, but not tired."

"Let me think."

"We should go to the dam," said Ba. "It is a full moon."

"So much energy?" said Bapuji.

Ba nodded.

Over his cotton homespun Bapuji wore a silver wool sweater, and on his head he wore a silver wool cap. Ba wrapped a beige shawl around her sari. The wind breathing in soughs around them, light from the moon dilute in the night, my grandparents looked elegant and otherworldly, spectral as they waited for an auto to arrive. It appeared from around the corner, its single headlight waxing then waning as the rickshaw accelerated and braked.

Near the handlebars, next to the images of Ganpathi and Durga, the driver had lodged a small radio. As the whir of the engine increased, he adjusted its volume upward, so that our trip, out of the city, to the reservoir, had a sound track. When the roads began to crowd — autos, scooters, motorbikes, and cars converging onto progressively larger thoroughfares — it seemed as if each vehicle birthed its own melody. As we made our way to the dam, I gauged our speed by how rapidly we passed by songs, or, conversely, by how quickly they passed us. I sat beside my grandparents, my mood light, and even the traffic, slowing everyone's progress, seemed to me less an irritation than a reminder of collective endeavor.

When we arrived, it was not to the sight of the reservoir but a parking lot. Disembarking, Ba paid the driver, who took her money without discussion. Then, slowly, we made our way from the parking lot along a path of packed earth that rose, broad and wide, up a hill covered by a dry scrub grass. The course was thick with people, most no more rushed than were we. In groups they ambled along, here a collection of boys of sixteen, seventeen, next to them a family, the young daughter riding on her father's shoulders. There were bands of schoolgirls and gatherings of family and friends, grandparents and grandchildren. Everyone had dressed for the occasion, in saris and *salwar kameezien*, in new blue jeans.

Sometimes, I'd notice somebody making his solitary way up the hill, but invariably, that person was alone only for a moment, an advance scout for or a laggard member of a larger assembly.

Cresting the hilltop, the path dissolved and opened onto an ample and gentle slope of grass and dirt. More than half a mile distant, at the incline's base, was the reservoir, and even more distant, its top barely discernible over the plate of water, was the dam. The colors of the place were muted and unclear and the landscape seemed frozen by the moonlight in the space between black-and-white and color.

The city had distributed itself less diffusely than was possible, so that the crowd was thickest closest to the water's edge and tapered to sparseness halfway up the slope. Walking down toward the water, Ba and Bapuji stopped and sat at a spot below the crowd's farthest edge but above its greatest density, a place where open ground seemed equaled by ground covered with sheets and blankets.

"We'll sit here?" asked Bapuji.

Ba nodded.

❀

The city had met because the moon was full; no justification beside the lunar was needed. The satellite lit the sky, and like an ancient people assembled to bear witness to a nighttime world revealed, we sat together without expectation of event. The moon's benevolence, our aggregation, this was the occasion. And though, to me, the night felt like the Fourth of July without the fireworks, both Ba and Bapuji were content to sit till the moon had almost set, considering the shadowy vista and their neighbors.

I left Bapuji and Ba and made my way into the spaces where people were dense. They had arranged themselves into interlocking bangles of humanity, in small circles or large circles, the rings abutting or, alternatively, passing one through the other. I made my way besides the water's edge, skirting the perimeters of these clusters.

The circles would shrink and expand as people joined, departed. The older people, it seemed, moved less, their family and friends shifting around them. Children were designated messengers, running in pairs from one group to deliver a piece of news to another, then returning, panting and happy. I looked in the circles for women my age and followed the fall of their hair, long and black, from their heads, down their backs. Most were married already, some tending to children that might have been their own.

From everywhere across the slope sprouted pockets of

music. There were the gentle coos of lullabies, mothers tapping their babies to sleep. There were the singsong rhythms of children's games. There were the sounds of *anthakshri,* where a person would sing a song, or a verse, and the person adjoining would identify the last sound from the person before him, the vowel or the consonant, and begin, with that as his guide, a new tune. Too, there were conversations and laughter that sounded, in that sonic landscape, musical. Wandering, I reached the edge of our celebration, and looking back into the assembly, marveled at the way one sound slipped into another.

"I haven't stayed awake this late for many years," said Bapuji after I returned. Ba lay on the blanket beside him. "When I was younger I hardly needed sleep. Rather, I didn't need it regularly. Some days I would be awake for hours on end, other times I would sleep through the whole day."

"I'm the same way," I said and Bapuji nodded.

"Your father was the same way." Then, "Your Ba is sleeping," he said. "I can tell from the way she breathes."

"Or snores."

"Or snores." He scratched his head, then smoothed his hair back down. He was sitting up and in the moonlight I noticed the thinness of his arms, and recalled that morning seeing the splotches of discoloration along their length, angry explosions of pigment he hid during the day under his white cotton shirts.

Dear Father and Mother, dear Chotuji, dear brothers and sisters, dear nieces and nephews,

Jai Shri Krishna!

I hope this letter finds you all in the best of health and spirits.

Some answers to your questions, first. I am doing well. If I seemed less than happy in my last letter it is perhaps because with Diwali passing, home felt very far away. But these feelings often depart soon after they arrive and I must remember to wait until my poorer moods pass before I sit down to write home as what I write on a particular day is the way you must imagine I feel for the weeks between my letters.

Likely, this note will answer questions from not your most recent letter (which I imagine is somewhere between India and America at this moment) but from the letter previous. I am sure you find this sort of communication as strange at times as I do, as though one were responding to an echo. As per the question of my financial resources, please do not worry. Matters are well in hand, as you will shortly see.

Doubtless, before you complete a reading of this letter, you will have seen the pictures I have enclosed. I will explain them soon enough, but first you must be wondering, "How did Vasant come by these photographs?" If I were to tell you that I took the snaps from my own camera, you would ask, "From where did Vasant acquire a camera?" Simply, I bought the camera from a store. More interestingly, I came by the money to make the purchase by teaching an American gentleman Hindi! The photographs are from an evening with this man and his wife during America's November holiday.

The gentleman, Mr. Joseph Goddard, is a friend of my advi-

sor. He has recently opened a venture in India. He will buy certain wood carvings from a supplier in Delhi and sell them as artwork to collectors in New York City. What manner of carvings? Mr. Goddard is collecting small Ganesh murtis, the sort that you can see in any house in the most backward of villages. More strangely, it seems the poorer the skill of the craftsmen, the more rough-hewn the idol, the higher price it receives in America. Mr. Goddard tells me that his customers feel that those carvings are considered more authentic by his buyers, as though skill in execution is not genuinely Indian. Were he speaking of the radios we build, or the cars, or the phonograph players, he might have a point, but at least in murti production, I felt compelled to tell him that we can do better than he is inclined to buy.

Mr. Goddard had mentioned his new business idea to Dr. Wolfenson, who spoke about me to him. The following evening, Mr. Goddard stopped by the laboratory and introduced himself. He asked if I would be willing to teach him Hindi. As a friend of my advisor's I would, of course, have agreed. Before I could agree to lessons, Mr. Goddard said that he would pay five dollars for each one-hour session. He wanted two lessons each week. Ten dollars each week for two months! Simply to speak Hindi! I tried to explain that such compensation was both unnecessary and excessive. But he said to me, "Hey, we are not in Russia here. You work an hour, you get paid for an hour." Who am I to argue geography and politics? I let him pay me.

On each Monday and Thursday, Mr. Goddard would collect me from my flat and I would go to his home. He has a beautiful house. His wife would cook us both dinner and then we would sit together and I would teach them Hindi. Mr. Goddard was not interested in learning the language rigorously. He was concerned only in acquiring a few phrases to be used in business transactions. When previously in India, as he tried to negotiate prices, the vendors would discuss in Hindi whether to accept his price, reject his price, or attempt to get him to pay a bit more. Mr. Goddard hoped the ability to follow their conversations would grant him an advantage. He is a clever businessman.

I began to teach him five weeks ago. He was so pleased with his progress that he invited me to his home during the November holiday. The evening before, I took the money I had collected from teaching and purchased a camera and film. The first few photos you have are of Mr. Goddard and his wife. The younger woman in the photograph is their daughter, Jennifer. She was at home for the holiday. Would you believe that during dinner, she asked me about the Upanishads? And the Gita also? It seems that at Smith College, where she is a student, she has taken a class on Eastern philosophy. We had a very good time speaking during dinner and because of her intelligence, I am not so embarrassed to say that on more than one occasion she seemed to know more than I about my own religion.

The other photos are as follows: There is one of Vijay and me in the common space of our apartment. You will all say that he is not heavy and you are correct. However, had I this camera ten months ago, I think you might have seen my earlier description was accurate. There is a photograph of New York City as it is seen from New Jersey, on its western side. Another snap is of my laboratory and Dr. Wolfenson. The woman sitting on the steps is Eveyln. There should be three frames of the college campus and two snaps of some buildings which were burned during this summer's rioting. They have still not been redone. The final photograph is of me in the new coat that I have purchased so that I may better face the winter season. I would have sent more photographs but I find that I am still a beginner when it comes to my camera and most of the shots I had hoped for are blurry and out of focus. Rest assured that as my skill improves, you will see America even more clearly. Please continue to write. My happiest days are when I see that something has come for me in the mail.

Love,

Vasant

Seven

A poplar sits along the front edge of my parents'
home and two broad and thick weeping willows sulk in
the recesses of the back yard. On either side of the
house, I know the boundaries of our property by the
differing heights of the neighbors' lawns, taller blades
on one side and shorter blades on the other. It was our
job, my brother and I, to keep the grass trim and shrubs
shapely, to rake away leaves in the fall, to spread fertil-
izer in spring, and it was my brother, the summer before I left for college, who discovered rot in the poplar.

My father called a tree surgeon to evaluate the tree
and the man, dressed in overalls and a green and yellow
John Deere hat, offered that it was probably best to
take the whole thing down. They agreed on a price and
a time and in the week intervening, my father took pictures of the tree, a full roll, twenty-four exposures. He
took photographs early in the morning. He'd stand beneath it and shoot film up into its branches. He'd take
photos from up and down the road and from the windows of the house that looked out onto it.

When the tree was cut down only the stump remained
and into this someone had drilled a series of long, deep
holes to facilitate decay. Each summer I came home, the
stump was a little less there, and when I returned home

after graduating from college, it had disappeared altogether. My father had covered the spot with topsoil and seed. A sparse new grass, the palest green, was growing.

After my father died, I had taken to looking in old albums and through stacks of photographs. Loose prints were ordered in two ways. Most sat inside envelopes upon which were written, in my mother's hand, things like, "Florida, December 1986," or "Poconos Camping, Summer 1984." A smaller number were held together in groups of ten or twenty by rubber bands, the banded photos pressed into six shoe boxes, divided from each other by index cards which identified neither date nor location, but onto which my father had scrawled titles and categories like "Front Yard Tree."

I went through the pictures my mother had arranged first. I recalled vacations and holidays and occasions, sometimes distinctly. Some photos reminded me of clothes—shirts and sweaters and pants—that had been favorites and had been outgrown or worn through or misplaced. I charted the arrival of my extended family, the pictures of them taken at the airport, then later around the house, during Thanksgiving and Christmas. In the photos my brother and I went from shorter to taller, my parents from young to old, our home from spare to busy then spare again, the seasons from winter to summer.

My father and I did not see much of each other that summer after my graduation. He would work until seven-thirty and when he came home for dinner, we'd all eat downstairs, watching the television. I'd slip from home soon after into the perfect smell and sounds of the night in that season, cut lawns and heaving woods.

It was only after I finished going through the sorted photographs that I bothered with the shoe boxes. I started with the pictures of the poplar, because they were first, and when I made my way through them, I looked at the next set, which my father had labeled "Groceries." The images were of a week's provisions, in bags in the trunk of his car, on the countertops of the kitchen, positioned in the refrigerator and arranged on shelves. There were pictures of laundry detergent contained in blue plastic bottles with ridged white caps, orange juice fortified with vitamins.

"This next one is our exit," I told Vasant.
"Then we are almost home," he said.
"Almost."

On the third of August we went out to celebrate my father's belated birthday. We had meant to go the day before but work had kept him late, past nine, so that by the time that he was home, his family had already eaten. But the next evening found us at a Mexican restaurant. My father, my brother, and I shared a pitcher of margaritas and my mother had a Diet Coke. We had nachos and enchiladas and a chile releño and toward the end of the meal, after my parents ordered coffee, my father caught me looking at my watch. "What are your plans tonight?" he asked. "Where will you go?"

"Some people are getting together."

"Which people?"

"You don't know them."

"Oh," he said. Then, "Why don't you cancel that plan and spend tonight at home? I was thinking we could look through some old slides. On the projector."

"I can't."

"My birthday night and you could not keep it free?" my father asked and my mother put her hand on his to quiet him. I thought to say something but decided to be quiet and my father said, "Well?"

"I kept yesterday open."

My father looked at my mother, his voice now quiet but bitter, and said, "Very American, this son of ours, very American."

I had almost finished the second shoe box when I found "Rajiv Sleeping." The series was tucked in between "Dodge Dart" and "Paving the Driveway." The photographs were taken at night, without a flash, and were of me, aged two or three, covers tucked around me or else thrown by my thrashing onto the floor, my body dim and small and cocooned in a one-piece yellow jumper as I slept. The photographs were in the apartment in which my parents had lived before they moved into their own home. Light from a hallway I don't remember warmed the room and my father's stills. When

I counted, I found that there were one hundred and eighteen photographs of my sleeping form.

The waiter came with coffee and because my father sensed my rush, he asked to see a dessert menu. He ordered something sweet and rich and asked for four spoons. By the time the confection had arrived, his anger had vanished, but his disappointment lingered. "These friends of yours cannot know you, *beta*. Raju, you cannot be who you are trying to be."

"That's a pleasant thing to say."

"I am trying to be helpful."

"It's not helping."

"You are not letting it. You don't understand how this place works."

"It works differently for different people."

"You think it will be different for you?" he asked and I nodded. "Be careful, be careful."

"How far is your place?"

"It's right around here."

"I hope I have not made you too late."

"Not at all."

"Your parents will be waiting for you?"

"Yes."

At home that night, before I headed out, there was a rattle on the front door. We have two front doors, one a screen door without a latch and the other a heavy and solid wood slab with a deadbolt lock. In the summer we keep the heavy door open and the screen door closed so the August night air washes in and out of our home, beneficent and tranquil and warm.

At the door that night was a neighbor with a petition. Some houses down, another neighbor had set his car on blocks. It had been up that way, at the end of his drive but covered with leaves and debris, visible to everyone walking by, for almost a year. The neighbor at our door thought the car an eyesore and he was collecting signatures in the hope that the other neighbor would be shamed into doing something with his decomposing jalopy. I answered the door and my father came down to the foyer after I'd called him. Our neighbor explained his case and my father agreed, yes, it was not so nice to look at, and yes, he would prefer if it were not there, but no, he didn't want to sign a petition or cause any trouble. When our neighbor left, he explained his demurral. "I know that man. There is nothing that will make him keep his car in such a state longer than if his Indian neighbor asks that it be taken down. And that man with the petition—some years ago his wife delivered a petition to our house. There were too many people living in this home, the petition said. This community is zoned for single-family dwellings only and that toad wanted to make trouble. So to hell with all of them and fuck that stupid car."

ii.

I told you I was feeling unsettled before I stole the Ambassador for my grandfather. Let me convince you. I had pulled the car from the turnpike onto the exit that Vasant's aunt had described. The ramp ended, I turned left, drove through an underpass, then on by three traffic lights. I passed a Getty station on my right and then a big red house with a long stone fence. I turned left onto an undulating road called Deer Run. A wooden mailbox shaped like a house marked the driveway to the home, a medium-sized Colonial, number 33, where Vasant's family waited for him. A pair of lights lit the porch; a stronger lamp cast a powerful beam down the length of the drive.

"Thank you so much for the ride," said Vasant.

"Not a problem at all. It was my pleasure. Really," I said.

We sat in the car. The weather had turned cooler, the coolness a catalyst. The day's rain, diffident, uncertain, was transmuted to snow, peaceable and steady and ghostly white. It fell from the sky slowly, more slowly than fat and angry drops plop from a thunderhead in the summer, more slowly, I think, than the return of bird sounds in the spring, than the autumn descent of leaves, dry and flaky, trailing from branches undressing to the earth.

"My baggage is in the boot."

"Right." I unlocked the doors, pulled a lever to open the trunk, and we stepped outside. The play of the headlights from my car with the lights from the house thickened and captured the falling snow and made it feel we were within a cloud: a billion microscopic ephemera of water hovering, shimmering about us. The driveway was beginning to cover. Set off to one side of the blacktop was a shovel, plastic red with a wood handle. Vasant picked it up. "This is for?"

"To clear the snow away."

"Like so?"

"That's it."

My legs felt unsteady beneath me, not in a clumsy, drunken way, but the way they feel after you have run a long way, your calves and thigh muscles lathered in lactic acid, weak, almost incompetent, the weight of the body to which they are attached too awesome a cumber.

Vasant removed his suitcases, setting them on the pavement beside him, and said, "I should take your address so that we can keep in touch."

"You're right." I leaned against the car and made my way to the glove compartment. I extracted a pen and a pad and wrote down my phone number and address in a frazzled hand.

❈

In the last conversation I had with him before he died, I meant to tell my father that I'd almost become a dad. We spoke on a Friday, and on the following Monday he was dead. I'd been meaning to call him since the Sunday before, when Anne had phoned me and explained what she had done. I had said I was sorry about the whole thing and asked if there was anything I could do. She had said yes, could I not call her until she called me? I said that would be fine.

Between that Sunday and that Friday I watched a lot of television. I watched late at night, my apartment dark except for the flickering light the set threw onto my walls, making everything I owned seem unearthly. I watched *The Andy Griffith Show* and *I Love Lucy* on Nick at Night.

On another night I rented a Hindi movie from an Indian grocery store. On the spine of the cassette the woman who owned the store had written the film's name in her own handwriting with a thick red marker.

In the movie two brothers are separated at birth when their mother dies. One is placed in a wealthy family, the other into a poor home. They grow up. The poor brother goes to work at the rich brother's factory. The manager, an evil-looking man with designs on the company, accuses the poor brother of stealing. The poor brother is fired and becomes despondent. He takes to the bottle. He meets a girl, poor also, but beautiful and honest. The girl's father is a cripple. The girl reforms the drunken brother. They devise a trap to catch the evil manager before he cheats the rich brother out of his company. They succeed.

As the rich brother is thanking the poor brother for his help, he notices a birthmark. It is a birthmark that he has also. It proves that they are twins. The rich brother gives the poor brother half his company. They manage it together. The poor brother marries the poor girl and brings her to his big new house. At the marriage, the girl's father stands, because the poor brother has paid for an operation to restore his legs.

I watched this movie twice, once at night, as I was falling asleep, and then again in the morning. I skipped class. I returned the movie and asked the woman at the store if she had a tape of the sound track. She didn't, but she recommended another movie, and I rented it.

When I called that Friday, my parents had just finished dinner. My mother and I spoke briefly, because she was washing dishes, and she passed the phone to my father. He asked about school and I told him, then I asked about work and he told me.

Then he said, "Something is bugging you."

"No."

"Tell me"

"There's nothing, Dad."

"What are you watching?"

"*Jeopardy*," I said.

"I can hear it in the background."

"What are you watching?"

"*Entertainment Tonight.*"

"Any news?"

"Somebody just got divorced."

"Who?"

"Someone in Hollywood."

Then we said good-bye. On Sunday it would snow and on Monday morning my father woke and started to shovel.

People die and are reborn. This is the way of the world; souls carom from one body into another, changing the old for the new. If in this life we are devout and spiritual, if we fulfill our obligations, if we do some good, we will return to the earth more blessed than we were before. I've known this since I was young, when I'd sit up, my back straight, each of my feet resting on the thigh opposite, and listen to pujas on the cassette player. In those days, we knew no proper pandit. So, as a substitute, my mother, my father, my brother, and I would sit in the third bedroom of our house, on the green carpet, concentrating on the murti that rested on our Kmart filing cabinet and listen to the *Satyanarayan Katha* as it played on the Sony Slimline. The cassette had been recorded in Hindi. There were occasional words that I could understand, words whose meaning was the same in Gujarati. The mass of the tape, though, was impenetrable, and this made it mysterious and powerful, the way conversations of adults are to children, the way that professional jargon intimidates the uninitiated. My mother and father would take turns explaining the narrative, familiarizing my brother and me with the unfamiliar sounds. As time passed, we both could tell from the rise and fall of the priest's voice, the changes in his diction, his occasional coughs, where in the puja we were, even while we never understood what exactly it was that the man was saying. We'd wait for the release of the *arti*, the conclusion of the puja when we'd again stand, sing a prayer, and, our backs bent, offer the light and heat of the oil lamp's flame in a clockwise motion to the murti. Then, finally, we'd eat the *prasad*, food we had offered to God for His blessing, food rich and sweet—milk with honey, wheat with sugar, butter and raisins, fruit salad.

The *katha* told five or six stories, of people who forgot God, who turned from him and were punished and then returned to him and were forgiven, their fortunes always taking a turn for the better. That improvement was the lesser reward; the more significant dividend was a rebirth into a sanctified position. Each of the characters in the stories was born into a body that provided direct service to an incarnation of Vishnu—one became a boatman for Ram—and this proximity to divinity was proof of consequence and justice, cosmic and eternal.

"But this *NY*, it means 'New York'?" asked Vasant after I had handed him the paper.

I nodded.

"I am confused," said Vasant. "I thought you were living in New Jersey, as well."

"Do you recognize the address?" I asked, smiling.

"No."

"I know who you are," I said.

"Excuse me?"

"I know who you are. Even if you don't, I do." Vasant looked nervous, like he'd been caught, I thought at the time.

"I don't follow."

"Mom is doing better. She's sad, but she's better. Some of the time she just wanders around the house and nobody can say anything to her, because she just isn't listening, but other times, she's good. Jaideep's doing well too. You know how he is—he's been distracting himself and keeping busy. He's getting by, though. He's going back to school. I couldn't handle that. I had to take the semester off. Do you know all this already? I don't know exactly how this works."

"What are you saying, Rajiv?" said Vasant, taking a step backward, stumbling over the snow shovel.

I wouldn't stop, though. "Boy, I guess I'm not handling things that well, Dad. I know I should, because I'm the eldest son and all, but I'd say I'm having a pretty rough time with it. I see you every night in my dreams. For fourteen nights in a row I've seen you and I want to talk, but I can't manage it. There are some things I need to tell you."

The front door to the house opened. Someone, Vasant's aunt, stepped out onto the porch and waved to us. She called to Vasant, "You made it here without difficulty?"

Vasant turned to wave back to her then turned to look at me. "Thank you again. I'll see you soon." I stepped forward to give him a hug, but he pulled away quickly, dragging his two suitcases behind him. He made his way to the porch and said something to his aunt, who showed him inside. They turned out the lamps beside the door. A few seconds later, the brighter, stronger light that lit the driveway was extinguished. I think I waited in the driveway awhile, longer than I should have, standing outside the car as it idled, its headlights on, the mist dispersing then renewing itself.

I drove home fast. Taillights appeared before me, headlights fell from the rearview mirror. I ran up close to cars in front of me till, scared, they shifted lanes and let me pass. I kept the radio off and heard the engine make a deep and satisfied sound. I noticed how the silver-white letters on the green exit boards shone. I shook free of whatever it was that had assaulted me.

I thought about Vasant, how he might tell his relatives across the world, or maybe years from now, his children, that when he first landed in America a madman received him at the airport and deposited him at his aunt's home. I thought about those things that are precious and about how we hold them. Always too close, so they blur, or too far, and they drift till they vanish.

iii.

We cremated my father on Thursday but waited till Saturday, when the weather had warmed and the Hudson had thawed, to dispose of his ashes. Early in the morning, the sunlight wispy and fresh, my family and I made our way to a Metro North station stop. We parked our cars in a near empty lot by the platform and walked around till we found a spot where some sleeping family's lawn sloped down to the water. Without ceremony, I tilted the urn I carried on its side. My father slid out. When he was in the water and I had righted the container, I looked down to see his floating dust defining the river's quivers. I thought for a while that my father would wash back up onto the shore, but part of him sank and the rest of him dispersed and I was thankful for small mercies. We drove back home, leaving the parking lot barren.

I'd saved a little bit of him, though, collecting a pinch of ash into a Ziploc bag and hiding the bag in my room. I don't know that I know why I did that. I'm a little horrified now to think of him in sandwich-bag plastic, nestled next to my socks like an eighth of weed, but anyway, there he was.

❖

The morning after dropping Vasant off in New Jersey I made it through brushing my teeth and showering before I thought of my father. I was rummaging for clothes when my hand brushed up against the bag. I remembered all at once that my father was dead and felt terrible and remorseful that it had taken a sack of ash to remind me.

During breakfast, I wrote a note to my mother, apologizing again for not calling to explain I would be late last night. I told her I met a friend from college at the airport, that we had talked, and that I had lost track of the time. She had waited up for me, the worry making her sick, and she cried from relief when she heard the garage door opening.

Without wanting to, I thought about Anne. I remembered how, when she'd said she preferred not to marry me, I'd felt first embarrassed more than I felt sad, how, later, the melancholy felt more serious than the shame. By the middle of October, I could go a stretch of hours without thinking about her; by the middle of November I could manage most of the day. Soon I'd meet women with her name and not even realize. She'd show up in my dreams the same way teachers from high school did—a curiosity. One day I might see an old photo and try to explain about her to someone who was interested but I wouldn't be sure about what had happened, not exactly. What month did I propose, how did she look, what movies did we see together, what did we say when we talked?

Then I thought about my father, dead, making his

way inexorably down the Hudson, past New York, into the Atlantic, shuttled by the ocean currents around the world, my father dead and tucked into my sock drawer. He'd fade just like she would, more slowly, but he'd go too. How would I remember him? He was left-handed. He worked in the yard wearing a white T-shirt under a green flannel. Around the house he wore this old pair of jeans from Sears that fit him funny. He liked his home fries crispy. On Sunday mornings he'd tune in to that New York radio station which once a week, from nine to noon, broadcast Hindi music and offered immigration advice. He thought there was proof in the Bhagavad-Gita that Indians, millennia before anybody else, had nuclear weapons. He liked the Miami Dolphins and Don Schula because he learned the game in seventy-two, the season they were perfect. He voted Democratic in every election but eighty-four. He was furious in eighty-seven when, the day his older sister would be arriving from India, my brother and I hadn't cleaned our rooms. He prayed every morning after he showered, ringing a small copper bell, and when he slept late, he'd compress his litany to a minute, delivering it accelerando.

I sat till past noon cataloging him. Some part of me was relentless and it kept thinking even though I knew I wanted to stop. In the end I was exhausted more than I was done. Feeling tired and desperate, I went upstairs and dug my father out of my drawer. I held him in my hands and then I held him up to the window so that where he had spread himself thinly, he was suffused with light. I heard a ringing that I thought was in my head but the answering machine picked up down the hall. My father's voice said, "You have reached the Kothari residence. We are unable to answer your call at this time. If you leave your name, number, and a brief message, we will return your call as soon as possible."

"Hello, hello!" There was a pause. "Hello, hello."

I ran to answer the phone. "Hello, Bapuji," I said.

"Raju, *beta*, how are you?"

"I'm fine, Bapuji, how are you?"

"Fine, fine. We are both fine."

"Good."

"Are you feeling well? Not too sad?"

"I'm doing okay. How about you?"

"Well, we are doing as well as can be expected."

"Good. Everyone here is doing the same, I guess. How is Ba?"

"She is fine also. She is asking for you, when will he visit?"

"Sometime soon, Bapuji."

"That is what you say each conversation. Yet you never visit."

"Maybe we'll all come soon."

"You come alone, don't wait for anyone else."

"Okay, I'll do my best."

"Don't just say okay! You think and you try to come."

"Yes, Bapuji."

"Good. Is your mother there?"

"She's at work. She started working again two days ago."

"Good for her. Tell her that we phoned and tell her that we have mailed a prayer book. Ask her to phone us back."

"I'll do that. Say hello to Ba."

"I will. Good-bye."

"'Bye."

That evening, because I needed to be away, I asked my mother if I could go to India for a while. She stared somewhere behind me and didn't answer. "Mom," I said. My mother, her eyes glassy and faraway, said, "Sorry, my mind was . . ." She stopped and started. Then, longingly, "I was just thinking of something else."

Dear Father and Mother,

Jai Shri Krishna!

Let me begin by apologizing. It was certainly not my intention to upset or anger you. I feel as though everything that I have done or said with a particular intention in mind is being understood in an entirely different way. I do see why you might perceive my actions in the way in which you do. Please allow me to explain myself more clearly, so this transcontinental confusion might be resolved.

Who are my people, you asked me. Let me answer. My people are Indians. I am Indian and this fact is not lost upon me even while I live away from my country. But if we are to say Indians are my people (and I have just said this very thing), we must also admit Americans are my neighbors. In my day-to-day life, it is with them that I interact and it is through them that I have been given these opportunities. When you asked, then, how it was that I could take the side of Mr. Goddard, an American, against my own people, these vendors of second-rate Ganpathis, the answer is not as clear to me as it seems to be to you. Am I to associate myself only with Indians? Does my allegiance to my country mean that I must side with Indians against Americans whenever the two are in a debate? Imagine, for a moment, my position. In a foreign land, I find a foreigner who invites me into his house, feeds me his food, provides me with funds I need to continue my education. In return, the man asks for a few words, so that he may interact more wisely with his business associates in India. Now, if those associates are dealing with him in honest and reputable ways, what harm comes from giving him the language, so that he can ease the worry from his mind? If, however, his associates are dealing with him in less than an honest manner, if he has offered them a fair price and they wish to exploit his ignorance for profit, does he not have an interest in knowing so? Is not some good served in this manner?

You wrote in your letter that I seemed to be serving my self-interest before considering the needs of my country. I must admit that I have difficulty connecting this single transaction to the undermining of my nation. Each action has its own implications, I understand this, but must all implications relate to India? Why can we not say simply that I taught a man Hindi, he paid me for that service, and along the course of the way we became friends? Why must each action be attached to seditious or patriotic intent? I wish I could remember more clearly what I had written, that I might point to those lines that had caused you such concern and say, "That is what I should not have written."

Despite my protest, I have, as per your request, taken a new position to replace my old one with Mr. Goddard. I have also terminated all discourse with Jennifer. I am sure she will think me rude.

I am now a shoe salesman. I spend six days a week staring at feet through the socks that cover them. There are people with tiny feet and people with big feet, people with clean socks and people with soiled socks, people whose feet smell as though they have never been washed and people who must bathe in perfume. I have made a game of these variations. I try to anticipate what kinds of feet people will have by looking at their faces and their manners of dress. I have no luck. People keep their feet secret and in disguise. My work is so dull that there are times that it seems I have spent a week with a single customer. Still, Father should take solace that India is unharmed.

Vasant

Eight

i.

Two mornings after the night spent under the moon we woke before the sun had risen because Bapuji had something he wanted me to see. The hill was small and barren, but in a flat town, it commanded a view. The abandoned civil lines sat at its base. Beyond that lay the road which we had just traveled, and beyond the road, the new city began in earnest, its closer buildings square and colored, the farther ones indistinct shades of dust and mud that faded indelibly into the flat and dry landscape surrounding. Bapuji found a spot for us to sit, big stones set off the road. The driver went to wander.

"These are the civil lines," said my grandfather. Below us were four main buildings, eight or nine smaller ones, clustered together and injured, connected by overgrown walks. Square and rectangular, red brick, large sections of their roofs had fallen in. Those walls still standing were daubed green with hints of plant life. The grounds of the complex were distinguished from the surrounding area by a low, and fractured stone wall, a tremor of a line, that was covered more often than not by scrub brush and earth. In the morning's early light, the place felt secret and remote.

"They are nothing to look at now, but in those days, this city was much smaller and there was but a single road that led here. When you arrived, you felt as though you were isolated from where you had come. Suddenly, white became the most prominent skin color and a person who was Indian felt he had arrived in an altogether different country.

"I came here to discuss a case with a civil service officer just after I had received my law degree and begun to teach. I was made to wait outside, in the middle of a summer day, for two hours. Not a drop of water was offered me. This place made you understand, rich or not rich, educated or illiterate, from the north or from the south, you could not be British so you must be second-class."

The air was dry, crisp. I listened to my grandfather and turned away from his face, craggy and serious. I looked at the buildings. I imagined them whole and reconstructed, populated by a people come to govern a foreign land. I began to see figures in the ruins. I imagined my grandfather, jilted, angry, sitting in this same place sixty years ago, dreaming of bombs and bridges.

But my reverie was broken because Bapuji said, his voice higher and sarcastic, "We have finally occupied their stronghold."

From one of the crumbling and broken buildings, over a fallen wall, a family emerged, a man and a woman, four children. I watched them for a moment, revealed by the new day. The bellies of the two youngest swelled preternaturally. This was no derelict site. Along a far wall ran a clothesline. Near the clothesline, a well-trod path led to a water pump. Two beaten bicycles lay against the wall of one of the larger buildings. Rubbish, new as well as old, was scattered around the area. After a moment, I saw another group of people, hidden in another crumbling building, their silhouettes crouched or in repose. After some more minutes of looking, it seemed the place was teeming silently in every place I hadn't looked, as busy, perhaps, as it had ever been.

"In India now, you can buy Coke and cellular phones. You can buy Pizza Hut pizza and Levi's jeans. Then, when we are all dressed in our new clothes, drinking our new drinks and eating our new foods, we can call each other on our new phones and be content. Perhaps on our way home from the beauty pageant, comfortable in our cars, we might throw a lamb burger from McDonald's to these children here, to set the world in order, because this is what we fought for, what we marched for, a properly modern country."

When the driver returned, he pushed the auto around onto the other side of the road. We climbed inside, Bapuji first, then me. The driver adjusted gears, twisting one handlebar. We were in neutral. The driver

released the brake. We coasted down the hill. The
driver saved gas. The wheels turned, slowly then
quickly. The sound of their movement compressed to a
hum. We spiraled down the hill. Our clothes fluttered
around our bodies. The hill ended and the driver
started the engine. We motored into town, through the
new section, then the old section, and then we were
home again.

There was an Ambassador parked in front of Bapuji's
apartment and inside, Chotuji was waiting for us. He
was wearing a safari suit, drinking tea Ba had warmed
for him. They were smiling and talking and they finished their conversation when Bapuji and I arrived.
Chotuji rose from his seat, to offer it to Bapuji, but Bapuji declined, moving instead into the bathroom. I sat
next to Ba on her bed.

"I come this early in the morning to hear you have already left!" said Chotuji.

"We both woke early and went for a walk," I said.

Bapuji emerged, having washed his hands and his
face.

"Take some tea," said Ba, passing a cup to her husband.

"Give it to Raju, I am fine." He moved into his room.

That day, I left with Chotuji in his car, his driver taking us to Ahmedabad. Chotuji had asked his brother if I
might not be free after all. Bapuji told him to take me,

that some pressing matters had come up, and that it was best that he saw to them himself.

We drove as quickly as we could manage and I wished the whole time we could go more slowly. The highway had one lane in either direction. When our driver wanted to pass slower vehicles he would sound his horn, which he had modified to play a tune, and edge into the lane opposite. He'd race around whatever was slowing him and turn quickly back into our lane, avoiding the oncoming traffic. Before each pass, the driver would nudge the car to his right, straddling both lanes of the highway, measuring the speed of the car in front of him, gauging the speed of the truck approaching, and I felt, each time, as though he were weighing our lives against his ego.

We had missed the first half of the match and when I apologized to Chotuji for making him late he told me not to worry, that if I hadn't come he wouldn't have come either. Our seats were good. The field's lawn was the greenest place in Gujarat. The whiteness of the players' uniforms was advertisement for bleach or detergent. The crowd was compressed into a thin, rising ring around the field. They cheered and groaned together. They pushed against one another.

When the match had ended we sat in Chotuji's car, idle and encircled by a swarm of happy spectators. And though the match was the equivalent of a minor league baseball game, I imagined the country watching and listening, captured in a skein of television towers and radio waves. I thought about matches, how they lodged themselves into the nation's collective consciousness. Years from now, in the countries to which they had emigrated, Indians might talk with each other about the cricket they had seen and the players they held in high esteem. Together, they would recollect events, and the feats would become greater with each telling and, despite the distortion, they would feel the people with whom they spoke knew them in intimate ways.

The restaurant we ate at that night was small and confined and Chotuji's mass was squeezed against our table. He perspired as he shifted, struggling for comfort, and he dabbed at his forehead with his handkerchief. Chotuji explained that he was happy he had retired. "Of course," he continued, "there are days I wish I were more busy. But I have time now. I mean to travel over the whole of India. There are holy places I would like to see. When we were younger, your grandfather and I made a great list of the places we would visit before we were old. Now we are both aged and we do not travel to each other's homes."

"Why is that?"

"I don't know."

"There must be some reason."

"When there are so many reasons it is almost as if there is no reason at all."

❀

On the way home from Ahmedabad, Chotuji told me another story about bombing bridges. In his tale, after the bombing the bomber flees his town without even returning home to his family or his bride. When his wife is arrested, and her release is offered in exchange for his capture, the bomber chooses to remain a fugitive, arguing that the nation is better served in this way. The bomber is almost caught when his brother, brought in for questioning, wilts after having had his jaw and his nose broken, and reveals his brother's location to the police. It is the brother who visits the bomber's wife those years she is held in prison, maintaining her spirits. In that same time, the bomber is ineffectual, never bombing another bridge, associating himself with groups ever angrier. When the bomber and his wife finally return to their hometown, years later, the brother helps him establish a new law practice, but for all his effort, it is only his failings that the bomber remembers.

The brother marries but loses his wife and infant child during a complicated delivery. He makes the bomber's family his own. Years pass and the brother's devotion—to the bomber, to the bomber's wife, to the bomber's children—is as unfailing as the bomber's criticism is ceaseless, because loyalty is the duty of a younger brother, as certainly as obedience is the duty of a son.

ii.

The next afternoon I could not decide if the day was warm or cool. When the breeze blew gently, wafting from one open window in through the rooms then out another, when the sun shone clean, I felt warmed. On those occasions when the wind gathered itself together and clouds obscured the sun for longer than just in passing, the hairs on my arms stood at attention and I would shiver as though I had been frightened into a fit.

Bapuji, dressed in white, sat in his room reading the newspaper. Ba and I played cards, both of us half considering a program on the television. Bapuji turned the pages of his paper, and the serial ended.

Ba drew a card and reconciled it with the others she held in her hand. She pulled at another, as if to discard it, before pushing it back into place. Her fingers moved across her hand twice more before, tapping with her middle finger, she settled on what was superfluous and threw it into the discard pile. It was of no use to me. I picked from the deck. The fourteen cards I held were mutually exclusive and unconnected in any fashion.

"See what else is on," suggested Ba. She tried to rub the arthritis out of her wrists as I rose from the floor and turned the set's dial, whirring from one station to the next. Ba said, "Slower," and then, deciding for the both of us, "Stop." We watched and played till, an hour not quite elapsed, the station disappeared, replaced by static. Ba looked at me. I shrugged and went to change channels, but everything was white noise.

"Maybe the cable is out," I said.

I turned off the television an half an hour later I turned it on again. Still nothing. Ba called to her husband in the next room. "Come look. I think the television is broken."

"The television is fine," said Bapuji, responding after a pause. "I canceled the cable signal." His newspaper rustled.

"What? Why?"

Bapuji stood in the doorway without a door that connected their two rooms. "We will still receive Doordarshan. The other channels are an indulgence."

"That machine is the only source of sound and motion in this house."

"It is neither real sound nor real motion."

"Better that than silence and stillness. Tomorrow you will go and have the signal replaced."

My grandfather tried, when his son was eleven years old, to teach my father to swim. Despite repeated lessons and assurances from Bapuji, however, my father, when left alone in the deep, would panic and sputter, then sink. Disheartened with my father's torturously slow progress, Bapuji, on a particularly warm summer afternoon, accelerated his education.

My father was eleven and had followed Bapuji to a

meeting with some landowner against whom my grand-father planned to file suit. The exchange between the landowner and my grandfather had gone poorly and Bapuji had become angry. My father was trailing his fa-ther, the both of them walking through the fields this man owned out to the main road, when they chanced upon a well. Perhaps four meters in diameter the well was busy with monkeys. They sat on the well's stone rim, eating fruit. My grandfather commented on what remarkable balance the monkeys had to be able to eat in such a precarious position. My father was unim-pressed and clambered onto the rim to duplicate their feat. The monkeys accommodated him without great concern as he positioned himself, his feet dangling above the water, his back to his father. Thus situated, Bapuji approached him, noted the proximity of a rope and the not too distant ripple of the water in the shaded dark below, and pushed.

My father fell ten feet and found himself surrounded by wet. Frantically he made his way to the wall of the well, finding gaps between the stones into which he jammed his fingers and supported himself. He began to yell. The monkeys above noticed the commotion and squawked in agreement. Curious, they arranged them-selves like Romans at the Coliseum, peering down at the spectacle.

Bapuji insisted that my father first swim across the length of the well before he would send down a rope. My father refused. They argued in this manner for nearly forty minutes, my father in the dark, wet and frightened, my grandfather in the light, warm and determined.

The monkeys grew disinterested and returned to their fruit. Finally, my father released the wall and pushed away a few inches. He treaded water for a moment and then reattached himself. Bapuji was not appeased and so, for the better part of the afternoon, my father spent incrementally more time away from the wall. When, much later, my father swam across the well and back to his spot, Bapuji let down some rope. Back on dry land, my father fumed. The whole way back, he refused to meet his father's eyes, restraining his own tears till he saw Ba and Chotuji on his return home. Then he cried and though Ba scolded Bapuji, my grandfather did not apologize.

Years later I would recall my father finding his way to water whenever it was practicable. His stroke was awkward, still it managed to keep him afloat. When I was seven, he had an aboveground pool installed in our backyard, circular, four feet deep the whole way round. On summer days after work, he'd swim till my mom called him into dinner, his fingers and toes prunelike and pickled, his skin smelling of chlorine, that suburban brine.

I caught Bapuji in my wallet that night. Without the television signal, my grandparents' apartment was quiet and by ten, the lights were out. I heard the stealthy rustle of my grandfather's theft an hour afterward. I watched him too, my eyes half open in the dark, as he reached into the back pocket of the trousers I had folded onto Ba's desk, extracting rupees and traveler's checks. I shifted in my feigned sleep and Bapuji froze. I shifted again and he scurried back to his room, prosperous.

When walking the next morning I opened my wallet to buy a soda, and finding it empty, complained to Bapuji.

"There are pickpockets all over this city, Raju," said my grandfather without pause. "We shall have to be more vigilant."

I asked, "Bapuji, what will you do with my money?"

"I thought you might have been awake."

We did not pass the jewelry stores and their window-display promises of a connubial Eden, nor were we near the market from which Ba each day procured the evening's victuals. There was nothing green in the place into which we walked and the sounds were all grinding and industrial and stung like kerosene inside my ears. Hungry-looking men twirled belts of lumber into chairs and tables, sawdust thick in the air they breathed. Nearby, laborers, their skins adulterated and metalline, coated by a fine patina of ore, made iron gears. Children with hammers knocked aluminum into thin sheets, bent right angles into copper pipes. Adjoining this industry was a small storefront without a sign and inside it was Bapuji's enterprise.

❋

Careful, even turns of the crank produced leaflets, their print not yet dry and prone to smudge, the paper saffron-colored and thin enough to see through. The sheets, printed in Gujarati, were inscrutable to me, but the characters were large and a cartoon placed onto the lower left corner of the page suggested caricature. Two men worked the doddered machine. They were dressed simply in sleeveless undershirts and dhotis. When Bapuji entered the room, the men rose to meet us, offering their *namastes* with dye-stained hands.

"Is this your shop?" I asked my grandfather.

"I share it with colleagues."

"You're printing a paper?"

Bapuji nodded. "And doing other things as well. I helped to build a school in UP, to train students for the IAS exam. We hire the teachers, we pay for the books, and the children have only to pray, to study, and to promise patriotism." My grandfather made himself clear. "You see, if we are not a proud Hindu nation, what are we? These government officials, they will make concessions to every minority possible, the Muslims, the backward castes, to win votes and they will admit any foreign company or church to make money. It must stop," he said, wagging a finger, "India must be governed for the benefit of its own people, not for invaders and parasites."

❋

"Servants of India, Soldiers of Ayodhya! Will You allow Foreigners to take Your Country from you? Will You allow them to replace Your Religion with Theirs? Will you close your eyes as Arab oil money buys Kashmir for Pakistan? You will Not! You must Not! Will You Stop the Western Missionaries who are Forcing Our People into Christianity? Gather this Christmas in Dangs and let Us Speak with One Voice! Hindustan is for the Hindus!"

Bapuji set the paper down and beamed.

"There is one thing more, Raju," said Bapuji, walking past the press. He opened a locked door at the store's rear and turned on a light switch. In the bare cement room an empty wooden crate stamped "Bharat Switches and Electronics" sat beside the door and a heavy burlap cloth covered something low and undulating, repeating in a pattern, across the rest of the eight-by-eight floor. My grandfather tried to bend at the waist but could not, so instead he sat down and, when well positioned, pulled up on the fabric and threw it back onto itself. "We will do some damage, Raju, this is assured."

The pipes were copper and plastic, sealed on both ends by epoxy or otherwise, by caps screwed on, tight and secure. Fuses extended from the centers of the plastic tubes and from the screw-cap edges of the metal ones. Two of the pipes had trip wire attached, slivers of wood holding the metal contacts apart, and two more lay half assembled, their innards empty and the mercury switches unattached. The devices were arranged in rows, six across, seven deep, on the cement floor, and to prevent them from rolling, small stones were placed around each bomb.

"How did you make these?" I said, trying to keep my voice steady, but I felt my mouth drying and my tongue becoming heavy.

My grandfather shook his head. "I bought them. I have a friend who makes fireworks."

"And what now?"

"What do you expect?"

"Someone will use them."

"Yes."

"We will hurt no one. It will be violence against property. At the time of his imprisonment, one of Gandhi's own magazines advocated such action. That is what started the campaign against bridges. Later they reversed that position and my activity became proscribed, but I do not think it was wrong.

"Raju, I need your help. We can begin to revitalize India. Things have been changing already, in the state and in the Centre, they are moving in our favor. These missionaries are forcing our tribal peoples to accept their gods. Think on the brazenness: fifty years after we throw them from our land, they return to begin again. I have helped organize a gathering in two days in Dangs of proud men, Hindu men, Indian men, and we will meet and make it clear that such behavior cannot stand. Come with me."

"Does Ba know?"

Bapuji nodded and then the corners of his mouth turned to the floor. "I have made your grandmother poor, Raju. Even now I steal away her money when she is not vigilant. I am unkind, Raju," said Bapuji.

"You aren't," I said and shook my head.

"I am. Your Ba is so thankful for small kindnesses and I am so poor in providing them. I have kept my wife from her children. I have sold away her home. I thought for years that she tolerated me because of affection, that she hung on each favor of mine so that they came somehow to equal my cruelties. Now, when I am frightened, I think that all that holds your grandmother to my side is routine and obligation."

I was silent.

"In America, your Ba would have divorced me long ago, but this is India. What is she to do?"

It should not have been enough to convince me. You will say I ought to have felt disdain or revulsion instead of pity or fraternity. But my grandfather, eighty-one years old, was warm, his arm crooked around my own. I felt the smallness of his skeleton and as he strode, it transmitted tiny, brittle tremors. We walked back home, passing places rich, then places squalid, the one making the other obscene.

It occurred to me that he was minor, eclipsed in this city of his—the place had outgrown him. And my grandfather would have known this, he would have understood it in a way that only a person who had aspired to significance might. His life's work he would have regarded as ineffectual. It was transforming, this impotence, morphing a secular man into a communal one, turning a labor lawyer against class reservations. He had lost those things he perhaps once hoped to hold dear, his children, his brother, his wife. He was destined soon for ash and he was in search of redemption.

Later that day, the dust in the air making the sunset a bloated and angry orange red, I thought about my father, infant and unguarded as he arrived in America, preserved in the mausoleum of Ba's tea tin. I thought of him without a community with which to surround himself, discovering a country, meeting its people, feeling as if the passing weeks measured a progression, time his ally.

But he had been sold a false bill of goods, and the country, she was less welcoming than she'd promised. My father would learn to work, not to provide, but to assure himself that he belonged. He'd bring his family over and, wide-eyed, they'd land at Kennedy, but month would follow month, and they'd struggle, with minimum wage and health insurance, with rent payments, with immigration lawyers, and ultimately it was all they could manage to cocoon themselves in their own company and watch Indian movies at home. He'd raise his children and they would learn to be disrespectful, to disagree, to shrink from his opinions. And when he'd try to warn them about America, how years after he'd arrived his passion went unrequited, his foreignness ultimately unforgivable, they would see that as his failure, not their country's.

It was only at night, though, when the house had fallen to sleep and I was still awake, that I decided. I thought about blastulas and gastrulas and morulas, about the knowing way in which cells unite and divide, only to discover that for all their precision they are unfit, because east and west are opposed on a compass, and this is natural law.

"Bapuji." I shook him. "Bapuji."

Waking, my grandfather turned on a lamp by his bedside and, the light reflecting gray and cloudy off the cataracts in his eyes, he sat up in bed. "What news, Raju?"

"I can help you," I said.

"Yes, you can."

iii

On Christmas Eve, early in the afternoon, I exchanged presents with Ba and Chotuji. I gave them both
cards. Ba gave me a blue-collared shirt and Chotuji
came by with a cricket bat signed by three members of
the national team. When a call from home came through,
I talked to my mother and then my brother. They wished
me a Merry Christmas and I wished them the same
while Bapuji sat witness, dour and glum.

We would not have had to steal the Ambassador had
I not become ill, but I began to perspire soon after dinner and felt a sudden, prickly heat creeping up my neck
and settling on my face. I felt flush and then I felt an
abrupt wave of nausea as my head went light. I went to
sit but became aware of an angry violence in my gut
and rushed to the bathroom, fearful of soiling myself.
The feeling continued for several hours and though I
took medicine, I felt near incontinent.

Bapuji and I were to board a bus late that night and
travel to the Dangs. The thought, though—of a long
and jarring trip aboard a bus without a toilet, a bus
stocked with people and their animals, prone to sudden
accelerations and turns, the bus driver and the passen-

gers indifferent to my infirmity, reluctant to pause as we careened through the Gujarat countryside—almost stopped us. I could not make such a trip, my bowels would not permit it, and Bapuji was reluctant to go without me to witness his greatness.

"Raju, can you walk for a while," my grandfather asked as I sat with Ba watching the television.

"Let him sit," said Ba. "He is not well."

"I can walk a little," I said to Bapuji.

"Come, then, the night air will do you good."

It was eleven o'clock and there were no women out, only men clustered around scooters in groups that felt vaguely menacing, and dogs. The murmur of television shows could be followed from one home to the next as we moved through the streets.

"We will have to leave tonight. We should arrive at the proper time tomorrow, or else we will miss everything."

"I can't take a bus, Bapuji."

"No, that will not work. It is too late to hire a taxi as well." A mutt was trailing us, mangy and hungry-looking. Bapuji yelled at it and it froze and he yelled again and it turned tail. We were alone on a cobblestone lane. Bapuji gathered himself. "There is a way."

We hired an auto to take us to Chotuji's home, but first we stopped at the shop Bapuji had rented. The in-

dustrial plots were deserted and when the driver killed
the auto's motor, the place was silent, the only sounds
those of Bapuji opening locks and opening doors. From
the back room, we took three crates of the bombs, leaving some twenty-five behind, and loaded them beneath
our feet in the rickshaw. Bapuji had swaddled the
bombs in raw cotton and when I asked him if it was safe
to be handling explosives, he said, "Not to worry, Raju.
One hundred and one percent safe."

A concrete wall, just taller than my head, anemic
pieces of broken glass set into its rounded top, bordered
Chotuji's compound, too treacherous to climb. Instead,
Bapuji walked to the gate and called the guard out.
"Hurry up, open the gate," he demanded. "Are you sleeping or are you drunk? I don't have the time to wait for
you. Move quickly." Recognizing his employer's brother,
anxious to avoid another scolding, the guard opened the
gate. "The keys, the keys, come on," said Bapuji.
  "Sir?"
  "The keys to the Ambassador, get them quickly, we
are late as is."
  The guard nodded and ran to the garage and back
out, producing the keys. Then he hesitated. "Sir, what is
this for, sir?"
  "My brother has explained it to you already. If you
are too stupid to understand, I won't explain again."
  The guard glanced at me. I looked less certain than
my grandfather.

"I need just a moment to check inside."

"My brother is sleeping. Will you wake him? Go quickly and open the gate so we can leave or my brother will hear of this later."

The guard scratched a spot just beyond his mustache. He changed his posture twice. His uniform began to chafe. His breath slowed and then he said, "Sir, I am sorry, but you understand." He turned quickly to escape, walking up the packed-dirt drive toward the house. My grandfather turned to look at me, desperate, his eyes proptotic.

Potted trees with broad green leaves flanked the guard as he approached the house, and it was into one of these that the man fell after I grabbed his *lathi* from him and swung the heavy-feeling rod as hard as I could manage across the back of his head.

I don't have any memory of fleeing Chotuji's compound but I recall feeling suddenly like there was traffic all around me. I tried to drive slowly and carefully but the car felt new to me. I had difficulty managing the gearshift, which protruded from the steering wheel like the control for windshield wipers. The clutch was stubborn. I couldn't approximate the Ambassador's dimensions well either and this left my grandfather and me in a perpetual state of imminent collision. Only my exaggerated jerks on the steering wheel and the alertness of other drivers on the road kept us from mishap.

When we left the city, the traffic eased. The highway was darkened. We passed cars that were not using their headlights. "To conserve their batteries," Bapuji said, "we should do the same." Twelve miles out, I saw the shape of a human form, sexless, lying across the road, portions of it flattened from previous tramplings, other parts seeming swollen in comparison. Our car bumped over it, as had the automobile in front of us, both vehicles indifferent. Bapuji said humorlessly, "Someone will not be coming home tonight."

The Dangs district sits at Gujarat's southern tip, a poorly drawn circle, thirty or forty miles wide. It is small and empty and covered by jungle and hills that progress into low mountains. In the whole area there are two towns to speak of, Ahwa and Waghai, and it was in the former of these, the district headquarters, that men began to amass on Christmas morning.

The town was already decorated in saffron—dyed strips of cloth had been tied around the town on the day previous—and the men, dressed in the same colors, carrying placards and tridents, passing out leaflets, gathered and angered after a late and heavy breakfast. They denounced church priests as thieves, explained how foreign funds threatened to convert the whole of India, demanded that missionary activity must stop. They garlanded sympathetic district officials. They shouted slogans and made speeches. The meeting dragged on, some of the four thousand participants growing distracted, talking to their neighbors, chewing betel nut and spitting red, runny saliva onto the ground, running to the bathroom, buying food.

The day was near its end when the stone-throwing began. A few minutes later the police charged, using tear gas and *lathis* to disperse the crowd. But smaller mobs formed, looting minority shops, stoning a missionary school. Converts were found later as the night progressed, alone and out on the streets, beaten. Two churches were set upon that night, and the following day, three more were set to flame.

Bapuji and I missed it all because he had fallen asleep and left me to drive. Two hours from home we were approaching Ahmedabad. Outside the city was an overturned truck, on its side, deserted. It had spilled its payload, large hoops of metal, their purposes inscrutable, onto the road. The cab seemed suspended in air, hovering over the embankment that sloped down from the highway. Along the edges of the truck were entreaties (Horn Please) and announcements (Public Carrier) and painted flowers and divinities rendered in plaster and plastic and assembled into dioramas attached to the roof.

I did not see the truck until we were upon it. I swerved and braked, the Ambassador crossing into the opposing lanes, then over edge of the road and down the dirt embankment till the front end of the car banged into a banyan tree's accessory trunk and steam from the engine released in a hiss up through the night air.

"Are you all right, Bapuji?"
"What have you done?"

"There was a truck in the road. I tried to avoid it."

"You cannot drive a simple car?" His eyes were wild.

"I'm sorry."

My grandfather balled his hands into fists and twice slammed his fists into his thighs. He glared at me and opened his mouth, looking as though he would begin to shout, and then closed it. He opened his fists and took my head between his hands. "Are you hurt, *beta?*" he asked, and when I shook my head no, he pulled me to his chest.

My grandfather, bruised, but not so badly, pulled out the cotton from one of the crates and piled the pipes from the other two into it, first pulling the fuse out of each except for one. When the fourteen bombs were gathered, my grandfather tied to the remaining fuse an additional length of coiled burn wire, sixty feet or so in length. "Go, Raju," he said. "Let us be rid of this."

I had, after the accident, turned the headlights of the Ambassador back on, and those beams illuminated the fields that stretched from the crash, a great beige flatness that slipped into a darkness that continued until the horizon. The tilled land, its furrows parallel and regular, looked as though an earthen ocean had been captured and stilled, a million low waves frozen like wrinkles on a photographed face.

I walked out into the fields for twenty minutes, till the headlights of the car were only a glimmer and the sound of cars passing on the highway did not reach me at all. Underfoot the dry ground crackled like a crust of snow breaking. I looked up into the sky, for stars, but the night was cloudy and the waning moon was hidden somewhere high and far away. I finally stopped at a ditch, setting the crate onto the ground. I called out to see that I was alone, and then unfurled the fuse, beating it a groove in which to travel with my heel. When the line had run out, I went back and checked it once again. Then I walked to its end, held a lit match to the fuse, and ran.

I spent the night in the Ambassador, awake, my grandfather leaning against me as he slept. It was not until morning that a passing tractor stopped for us, and leaving behind the carcass of Chotuji's car, we rode it to the next town, from where we placed a phone call and, later, caught a bus home.

iv.

Two days later, leaving Ba and Bapuji, I reconsidered my arrival in India. That mid-December night, a second cousin and her husband had collected me at the Sahar International in a small, blue Maruti-Suzuki hatchback (not quite a Yugo, but not quite a Civic). Coercing the car into receiving our three bodies and my three bags, we sped from the airport at an indeterminate speed, in an indeterminate direction, into the early autumn feeling late Mumbai winter night. The city met and then left the car in a blur, leaving only the impression of a giant place, spent and collectively asleep, inside in homes, outside, along sidewalks, in hovels that lined the road and blurred distinctions between the two.

My flight had been delayed for eleven hours. Running late, we drove directly from the airport to the Victoria Terminus railhead to meet my connecting train. At this hour, when perhaps the exhausted station would have benefited from a softer, more forgiving glow, its interior world was instead crystalized, lit by harsh, fluorescent light. Garbage littered the platforms and the tracks in so profligate a way the mess seemed the product of some intentional effort. Urchins and coolies rested in the mess, under the lights, their arms thrown over their eyes, transparent sheets over their bodies for warmth. Lone passengers sat on their luggage defensively and families leaned on one another in a light and uncomfortable sleep. For us all, travel, despite whatever excitement might await at journey's end, was at this hour miserable.

In the morning, though, eight hours from Mumbai, I spent the better part of what remained of my trip staring out the window at the countryside. The train's clackety-clack and creak, an abrasive sound in the city, transformed in this more rural context to a kind and romantic meter. When the train stretched round a curve I saw its red-yellow cars in a swift, clean arc and was impressed by the same enterprise of travel that hours ago had seemed lifeless; I imagined us to be a convoy of mobile villages, twenty cars of people, rushing through space.

Outside the train, the fields were flat, an earthy, fertile brown, and above the sun was shining with winter's restraint. Livestock, cows and bulls and water buffalo that had long since learned to ignore the passing of trains, rested alone or stood together in groups that seemed modestly social. Because I ignored other sights, of cars and roads, of power lines and satellite dishes, of thin, thin children, I experienced the scene as pastoral in a way that was willfully ignorant, and I was refreshed.

❈

Ba saw me to the station. We followed the same route, in reverse, that I had taken when I arrived. But because we traveled it in the early morning instead of the early afternoon, it felt different—pacific and becalmed. Floating through the quiet, my grandmother held my hands between her own. Their backs were thickly veined, her fingers knotted with the swelling of age.

Earlier I'd asked her if she would come to America. "There is that hope," she had said, but in the next room we both heard Bapuji lingering over his prayers, savoring the fullness of Sanskrit syllables.

"You should try," I'd said and Ba had nodded.

My grandfather excused himself from a trip to the station. At breakfast, dipping his biscuit into his tea, he'd mentioned pressing matters that required his presence. Neither Ba nor I protested. I asked him when I would see him again.

"You will come here before leaving for America?"

"No."

"Then maybe your Ba and I will take a trip to Delhi to see you off. Today I am busy, but we will see to it that we meet you before you go."

"Really?"

"Ninety-nine percent," said Bapuji.

I was leaving them prematurely, bound by train to Delhi and from there to Kanpur. I was to meet my aunt, my mother's sister and her family, and then I would

leave for home. Ba had phoned Chotuji and he had secured me a compartment on the train through an associate in the rail service. We arrived an hour early and
she sat with me, waiting for the engine's warning whis-
tles and the telling shudder of departure.

"The guard is all right?"

"No lasting damage."

"Will you tell Chotuji again that I am sorry?"

"He is not angry."

"Still."

"I will tell him. You should write him a letter." Then,
passing me a plastic bag full of mango juice boxes and
lunch, Ba said, "I have packed food for the trip."

"Thank you."

"Don't worry so much," she said.

"I won't."

"We will be fine."

"I know it."

When the train left the station, I saw Ba, the white sari
draped across the white hair on her head, diminish and
then disappear. Then I lost sight of the platform and after that the town. Soon I was in another place entirely.

The train was regular in its departure but its speed
out of the station was slow then fast then slow again.
Time and corresponding landscapes passed unevenly
until I reached Bapuji's bridge. It is a massive construction. Months removed from the monsoons, the river below had collapsed to a trickle. The exposed bed, wide,

was dry but not cracked. From scattered puddles, ener-vated oases, plants fresh and green, stained the brown with color, and women, occasionally shiny with hints of gold thread, beat clothes by the water, knocking the dirt out of them with wooden paddles. In the flats surround-ing, boys flew paper-thin purple kites that seemed more connected to sky than string. In truth, the river looked benign and the bridge, spanning a torrent that did not exist, was ridiculous.

I'd thought for a while, till just after I drove the Am-bassador off the road, really, that the theft was selfless. Three days later, it is clear to me that I stole the car, cracked open a man's skull, for myself, to settle the riot in my head.

There are stories that we tell ourselves, I think, about the people we know and the people we are. We under-stand ourselves best through a rough triangulation, fix-ing our locations by knowing first where it is our familiars are rooted. Start changing recitals, start shuf-fling around points that need to be immovable, shift the north star, and see if you don't lose your sense of direc-tion, drive off the road into a tree, mistake a stranger for your father.

My grandfather and his son were for me poles, lo-cated as far from each other in my mind as they were separated geographically. The one was audacious, im-pudent even, the other chary. My grandfather was clas-sic, in the way of old film actors and actresses, captured on celluloid in poses smooth and effortless; my father tabloid in the ways his frailties were exposed and raw. It was clear to me the ways in which they might be ordered and graded. But it turns out the way in which I make people convenient, my habit of condensing lives to easy comment, is a poor means to navigate, because people fracture into possibility, they regress relentlessly into labyrinths which are personal and unknowable.

It is effortless, though, an easy exercise to understand people in that dishonest way where the part anticipates the whole. It is the manner in which we decide an immigrant's accent reveals his foreignness, that accidents of pigment confer fraternity, that stealing a car is closer to heroism than sad farce, in which by damnations, a grandson tries to secure redemption for his grandfather.

It is the way in which I came to understand my father. He was without temerity, timid and inept; he was forever awkward because he was misplaced in America and his fate would not be my own. I would not allow that my father had been brave and open in ways that were remarkable, that his immigration was heroic; it was great and terrible and it was persistently hopeful, undertaken in the light of that grace which says that worlds might meet and join so that both are altered in ways sublime and transcendent. To make that admission was to suppose America might treat us similarly; my father's frustrations might presage my own.

But it is difficult to think in any other way; I am realizing this as my head works itself to exhaustion. I'm unsure how to choose now, tomorrow, allegiances, nations, between loves which refuse to reconcile themselves.

So, while I try and get things straight, ask me about people and I'll tell you plain, uncomplicated things. My proposal failed because Indians and Americans do not mix, not because of Anne's peculiarities or my own. My grandmother is loyal, not tethered and kind and seasoned, not defeated, not heartbroken. Bapuji is a patriot, my childhood hero, not an aggrieved old man, never twisted or impotent.

My father is dead, but gloriously departed, an immigrant who resettled his family so that they might live better than he had. He didn't have a paunch. He wasn't balding or quick to anger. We occupied similar worlds. Winter was a wonderland. His adopted country had welcomed him; their embrace was sustained passion.

Respected Father and Mother,

I have addressed this letter to Pa at his office, thinking that it is best that he reads it first. I leave it to his discretion to pass on the information it contains at his convenience. Let me begin by saying that I am well except for my longing for home. I hope this letter finds you all in the best of health and spirits.

To the point, then: I spoke with Mr. Mehta this morning. My advisor allowed me the phone call from his office and I received the connection without any problem. Mr. Mehta seems like a good man. He was kind over the phone and generous in his job offer. I am certainly thankful for the work Pa has done on my behalf to secure a position for me, and the company seems good by Indian standards. However, and I do not mean to seem un-grateful, I feel that I would not be well served working for his firm. I apologize if this causes any inconvenience for Pa.

Your next question must be, "If Vasant has refused this job, if this job does not serve Vasant well, it must be because he has a job with brighter prospects." This is true, you will be happy to know, but the situation is more difficult than just this. Follow-ing Pa's advice, I wrote letters of inquiry to a number of firms in India. Surprisingly, I received encouraging replies from almost all of them. In this matter, credit must be given to Chotu cha-cha, as this was his prediction concerning the value of an Amer-ican degree. With the letters of inquiry to the companies in India, I also, on my thesis advisor's advice, sent out letters to a number of businesses in the United States.

I know your reaction even now. "What need to send letters to places in the United States? Vasant agreed that after his school-ing was finished he would return to India." Let me say, I have not forgotten my promise. I will not stay in America, but all the same, I may holiday in this country a bit longer. "Words games," you are thinking. I assure you that they are not. I cannot see myself staying too long in this country. All the same, I would be foolish to think I could use any of what I have learned here at home. My degree would be only pageantry. India cannot sustain the kind of work that I have become accustomed to doing.

"Even if you can use your education better in America, to what end, or more correctly, when will it end?" Tell me, in your next letter, if I have anticipated your concerns accurately. To what end is simple. Imagine—here I am able to find things, to do things, first, before anyone else in the world. In India, every job I have been offered is trying to make something, and make something shoddily at that, that they have been making here for twenty years. There is more money here and I can be better compensated for the work I do. There is better engineering here and I enjoy being a better engineer.

"But," you will say, "this does not answer the question of when. When will you come home?" This is a bit of a delicate question. Let me approach it in this way. It is nearing summer in Newark, the spring is ending. Today the weather was warm in anticipation of the coming months, not so hot as it is at home, but warm enough that the whole city was uncomfortable before they expected to be so. What to do? As I was walking home this afternoon I reached my street and watched children open a water valve that rose from the street with a wrench. The pressure from the valve made a fountain to play inside. I watched the children run through the water. A boy from my building convinced me to join him.

I set down my books. I took my shirt off my chest and my glasses off my face. The water was so cold, perfect for a perspiring student, and I soaked myself. It was like waking for a second time on the same day.

When something remarkable does not happen in the laboratory, or in my classes, something magical occurs all the same. I know what you are thinking, that the novelty of the new is something that can only entertain for a short while. I know this. So let me stay in this place, let me take this job for two or three years, and when I find it has grown uninteresting, as you know it must, I will come home. I'll wait on your letter.

Your loving son,

Vasant

About the Author

Sameer Parekh was born in Poughkeepsie, New York. He attended Brown University and was a 1996 Fulbright Scholar to India. He is currently a physician in Boston, Massachusetts.

STEALING THE AMBASSADOR

DISCUSSION POINTS

1. Discuss the significance of the William Kennedy quote at the beginning of *Stealing the Ambassador*. Why do you think Parekh chose it to frame this story? What do you think "I liked all their lies best, for I think they are the brightest part of anybody's history" refers to?

2. Look at the opening prologue, which begins, "There's an old story in my family. . . ." Consider it in light of the entire book. Examine how the author manages to distill the essence of the entire book into a few pages. How does the opening set up your expectations as a reader? Do you think the narrator "became a thief for a cause, for the story" (page 11)? Why?

3. The narrator's father's name appears for the first time on page 34, and the narrator's much later. What are some of the reasons the author keeps the characters' names out of the text for so many pages? How does this affect the reader? What does it do to the story as a whole?

4. Were you surprised that Rajiv's mother had been lied to about her medical school entrance exam (page 25)? What is your reaction to her father's lying about it? Explore the cultural implications of this lie, and the significance of her Indian-born American husband being incensed by the whole situation. Look at page 39, when the narrator says of her mother that she "couldn't be a doctor, she understood that her marks weren't good enough." Considering the impact of the choices a person makes (or those that are made for one) in life, how did the father's lie affect her life?

5. How does Parekh's use of English and the family's native Indian dialect affect your perception of the characters? How does it affect your sense of place and time and society? How does the phrasing and placement of certain Indian words flesh out the characters?

6. Look at the grandfather's story on page 62 that begins, "Listen." Why did the author place it at this point in the book? What is the story's importance?

7. Examine the letters from the narrator's father that end each chapter. How do these color the book's narrative? What do they reveal

about the immigrant struggle to balance—and reconcile—the new life with the old?

8. What was your first impression of the narrator's attraction to the young Vasant in the airport? Looking at the narrator's interpretation of reincarnation on page 225, do you believe that the young Vasant really is the narrator's father? Are there any other reasons, besides his belief in reincarnation, that Rajiv thought Vasant was his father? How does this belief affect Rajiv's life? What are your feelings about reincarnation in your own life?

9. Parekh shifts back and forth in time and place throughout *Stealing the Ambassador*. Look at a couple of places where this happens and, keeping voice and language in mind, discuss how the author makes these shifts clear. Were you able to follow the story? Explore whether or not these shifts mirror the narrator's train of thought. Why do you think the author used this technique? Share whether or not you think this is an effective method for this book.

10. On page 118, Rajiv talks about his thirteenth birthday. What does this story reveal about his father, and about the roles we play in our family?

11. If you are an immigrant, or know someone who is, what is your reaction to the narrator's "feeling as though situated in a demilitarized zone" (page 121)? Looking at pages 138 and 139, beginning with "I was struck that morning . . . ," and also at page 179, "This was part of our immigrant canon . . . ," discuss your interpretation of what the author is saying. Do you feel these are common themes for immigrants? Share some of your own family lore about coming to America and how it is or is not similar to Rajiv's family's experiences.

12. Discuss the significance of the story about the robin on page 180. What is going on at this point in the story, and why is it placed at this particular moment?

13. Look at the grandfather's speech on page 241, "In India now, you can buy Coke . . ." Why is this important? Does it add a different perspective on the difference between East and West? Talk about how this may shed some light on the grandfather's political involvement and interests.

14. Why does the grandfather's brother tell Rajiv his version of the bombing of the bridges (page 245)? Does this change Rajiv's impression of his grandfather? For example, on page 255, Rajiv seems to be reevaluating his grandfather when he says, "It occurred to me . . ." Could he have seen or understood this about his grandfather before his uncle's speech? What does this reveal about the nature of history and family lore? Does this relate to the opening quote by Kennedy?

15. What is the significance, and symbolism, of Rajiv's stealing the Ambassador? Share whether or not you think it's a good title for the book, and why.

Discover more reading group guides and download them for free at
www.simonsays.com.